DEVIL
YOU
KNOW

KelpiesTeen is an imprint of Floris Books
First published in 2015 by Floris Books

The publisher acknowledges subsidy from
Creative Scotland towards the publication of this volume

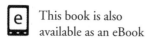 This book is also
available as an eBook

British Library CIP data available
ISBN 978-178250-179-4
Printed in Poland

DEVIL YOU KNOW

CATHY MACPHAIL

KELPIESTEEN

FOR ROBERT, ROSS, DANIEL, REBEKAH, JESSICA AND ISLA ROSE

//CAMERA 0290

My name is Logan,
Logan Massie, and this is my story.

ONE

I'm telling it from the time it seemed to begin, for me anyway. A warm night in August. I stormed out of our flat in Glasgow, angry, frustrated after yet another argument with my mum.

Baz was waiting for me when I left the house. He was leaning on his elbows over the walkway, all dressed in black. His joggy trousers, his hoodie, even his trainers were black. He always dressed in black. I would joke with him that in the dark he would be invisible until he smiled. His teeth gleamed white against his tanned skin.

"I think you spend half your time under a sun lamp," I would say to him.

And he would laugh. "Spanish blood, my friend. My grandfather was a Catalan."

I never knew if that was true. He was always making stuff up, seeing whether I'd believe it or not. I usually did.

I think I was the only one who was ever allowed to joke with him that way. He would never have taken it from anyone else.

Why were we friends? I often wondered – I always thought he was so cool, and cool was something no one would call me. We just seemed to click from the first time we met when I came here from Aberdeen.

He turned when he heard my feet pounding along the walkway. "You had another fight." He nodded towards my flat. Had he heard my mum yelling at me, and me yelling back? Probably.

I nodded. "Sick of it," I said. "All we ever seem to do nowadays is argue."

"Lucky you've got a mum," he said. "Mine dumped me. Took one look at my backside, thought it was my face and did a runner." He always made a joke of it. But I don't think he really felt it was funny at all.

Some old aunt and uncle had taken him in – his 'Auntie Dorothy', he called her. His uncle was always just his 'Unc'. They seemed fond of him, he never had a bad word to say about them, but they didn't give him any rules. He was able to go where he pleased, and could stay out as long as he wanted.

"Come on," he said, pulling me on.

"Where are we going?"

"See what's happening."

It felt good running through the streets of the estate with Baz. He was the same age as me, but a lot taller. He already had a reputation as a bit of a hard case, tough, scared of nothing, a bit dangerous. Some people even said he had something missing 'up here' and they would tap their heads. I'd seen them do it. Of course they only did that behind his back. They would never have said it to his face – or they would never have said it twice.

But Baz had only been a good friend to me since I came here to Glasgow. I hadn't wanted to come. I liked where we lived in Aberdeen. My life had always been there. I had friends there. It was my mum and her new boyfriend, Vince, that decided we should move, and to here of all places, to a three-storey block of flats in a sprawling, run-down estate. I'm not good at mixing anyway, but here I'd felt alone, out of place, like an alien in a strange new world, a small-town boy in the big city. I was called names because of my ginger hair, and my accent.

It didn't take me long to find out – the hard way – that words can mean different things in different places. The first time I called a boy a 'loon', he was ready to floor me. But that's what we call boys up there in Aberdeen. A boy is a loon, and a girl is a quine. This boy was not prepared to listen to that explanation. He was sure I had insulted him. He had me by the throat, ready to do me serious damage. And then, Baz stepped in. The first time I'd met him. He told the boy to back off, and the boy did. He looked really scared of Baz, moving back at once as if he could see this was someone to be wary of. I realised then, this was the kind of boy I wanted as a friend. Everyone listened to him, seemed a bit afraid of him too. And since I had met Baz, no one had ever called me names.

TWO

I think Baz was as much of an outsider as I was. But at least he had a few friends. And his friends became mine. They were there waiting for us at the shopping precinct, sitting on a wall just outside the Turkish takeaway. Claude was there, and Gary, and Mickey. Mickey had his dog with him. He usually did have his dog with him. 'Ricky', he called it. That made me laugh the first time he told me.

"Your name is Mickey, and you called your dog Ricky? What were you thinking about?"

"I was only three when I got him! What did I know?" But he laughed too when he said it, used to people making fun of their names. How he loved that scabby dog of his – it looked like a cross between a mangy werewolf and a ferret, but you would have thought it was a Royal Corgi the way Mickey treated it.

The boys stood up when they saw us coming. They weren't too sure about Baz, afraid of him maybe. At least that's what I always thought. Yet I think, like me, in spite of that fear, they wanted him as their friend.

"What's happening?" I asked.

"Nothing much," Claude answered. Claude Handley was overweight, that's what we said to his face. Behind his back we admitted he was just fat. 'He'd give a tub of lard a bad name,' Baz would say.

Claude couldn't talk without swearing. I suppose we all swore. Thought it was cool. But with Claude, every second word was a swear word. He even broke up words so he could swear, like, 'Nobody better call me over-$!!%in'-weight!'

So what he actually answered was, "Nothing $!!%in much," if you know what I mean.

I'm not using the swear words here, because I've been asked to write this down. I don't know who is going to read it. But when I'm writing down what Claude says, even sometimes what the rest of us say, you can remember to put in your own swear words.

"Anybody got any money?" Baz asked.

They all hesitated. I think they were worried Baz was going to ask them for some. We all knew he wasn't good at parting with his own money.

"Don't worry," I said, pulling out my pockets. "I'm skint as well."

Claude kicked the ground. "Always skint. Sick of that." (Remember, put in your own swearing.)

"Maybe we should get a job," Mickey suggested.

"A wee paper round," I said. "Something easy."

"Yeah, delivering papers up to a twenty-storey flat... with the lift broke," then Baz laughed and began to wheeze as if he was out of breath. "Haaa... been there... haaa... done that."

"We could wash cars," Claude said. "Charge a fiver each car. Wash, dry and polish."

"Boy scouts do it for nothing," Gary reminded us. "For charity."

Gary Balfour was definitely the good-looking one. A lock of brown hair always hung over his huge brown eyes, and when he flicked it back, girls swooned. We were always telling him he should audition for a boy band. He would walk it.

"But I can't sing," he would say.

"Neither can they," Baz had told him, and we all laughed.

Girls were always checking Gary out. I saw a couple of them right then, coming out of the takeaway, glancing over at him and giggling. Gary ignored them, and that seemed to make them like him all the more. Girls are funny that way. He held out a tenner to us. "Well boys, Gary to the rescue. My old man gave me this. And this."

He plucked at the collar of the leather jacket he was wearing. Gary was always in designer gear.

"Did it fall off the back of a lorry?" Baz asked. Most of the things Gary's dad got did fall off the back of a lorry. His dad was well known in the area as the man who could get you anything you wanted, cut price.

Gary stared at the ground for a moment. I think he would have snapped something back, if he hadn't remembered Baz, crazy Baz. Instead, his face broke into a grin. "Must have fell off the back of a Merc. My dad only gets the best."

They all laughed. So did I. I was glad to be friends with them. But I was sure they were only friends with me because of Baz. He'd been there first, a kind of leader, though they would never admit to that. Not to having a leader. We were a crowd of boys who were friends. Not a gang that needed a leader. Though there were plenty of gangs around here like that. I'd heard about them. But Baz was our leader, no doubt in my mind about that. I'd seen it. How Baz could make the boys do things, manipulate them. Make them think it was their idea in the first place. He was clever that way. What Baz wanted he usually got. Yet, they liked him, just as I did. When Baz was good, he was great. Funny, and always full of ideas for things to do.

Not that night though. After Gary had bought us all chips with his tenner, we had no money to go anywhere and we spent a boring couple of hours just hanging about the shopping precinct, throwing chips for Mickey's dog. Not that he ate them of course. He'd drop them at our feet and wait for us to throw another one. According to Mickey, Ricky was very fussy about what he ate.

"He's used to chops and steak mince," he told us. "He's better fed than me."

That night, Ricky was our entertainment.

"Nothing ever happens in this dump," Claude complained when we were all ready to go home.

And I always look back and think that was the last time we could really say, 'Nothing ever happens'. What happened the next night sent a line of dominos crashing down that toppled into a nightmare.

THREE

Mum didn't like me hanging around with the boys, even though she'd never met any of them. Next night while we were having our tea she started harping on about them again. "I don't like the thought of you with a gang," she said.

When we'd first come here she'd been told about the gangs who roamed this estate. She was always warning me to keep away from them.

"We're not a gang," I told her. "Just a bunch of boys looking for something to do at night."

"It's what you might be doing that worries me."

"They're a good bunch of guys," I said.

"Why don't you bring them here some night?"

She was always asking me to bring my friends to the house. She wanted to meet them she said. I knew what she really wanted. She wanted to check them out, make sure they were suitable, thinking of the not-so-suitable friends I had made in Aberdeen. But just imagine me saying, 'Oh let's meet up at my house. My mum wants to meet you.' Like a bunch of girls having a sleepover. We weren't those kind of friends.

"What do you think we are: the Famous Five? 'Why don't you all come to my house for tea and lashings of ginger beer?'" Once, I'd been able to make her laugh when I said things like that in a fake posh voice. I used to read all the time, and the Famous Five were some of the first books I remember. And her favourites when she was a young girl, she had told me. But she didn't see the funny side of it any more.

I was trying to remember the time Mum and I'd been good together, when we used to laugh together, before Dad had... before he had... No, I still couldn't even say the word. He was gone. Forever. I had to face up to that, but it still hurt so much to know he would never come back. We used to be a family, me and Mum and Dad, we once all got on so well. She'd been a fun mum, till we'd lost Dad. Now, she was no fun at all.

No use thinking of that now. I snapped my mind back to the present.

"We're not doing anything bad. Why do you always think the worst of me?" I sounded angrier than I felt. I know I did. It seemed we never could have a conversation any more. Just arguments.

Her boyfriend, Vince, him of the army crew cut and the tattoos (honest, I've never seen a man with so many tattoos), came in from the kitchen then. He'd heard my raised voice. He looked from her to me. "Hope it stays that way, Logan. Once you get caught up in these things it's hard getting out. I know, Logan. I was in a gang when I was a boy."

Yeah, I thought, *probably the leader*. I was waiting for him to say it, boasting as usual.

"You end up doing things you don't want to do, but you don't know how to say no. You stay well away from trouble, Logan."

"What are you saying that to me for?" Vince always annoyed me so much. I couldn't help feeling like that about him. It was because of him that we'd moved down here. He was a Glasgow man, he had told us. So we had left everything behind and followed him here. He had a son, Andy, who was nineteen. He was away now, thank goodness, doing his training to be a soldier, like his dad. My mum was besotted with Vince, ever since she met him. He said 'Jump' and she asked 'How high?' Always put him first. Why didn't she ever stick up for me?

She only put her hand on her boyfriend's arm. (Boyfriend! Imagine a woman her age having a boyfriend!)

"Leave it be, Vince," she said. "Logan's going to keep out of trouble. Aren't you, son?"

She said it as if I was always *in* trouble. "You have such faith in me, Mum." I refused to even look at Vince.

He answered me as if I had. "We do have faith in you." Vince sighed when he said it, as if he was tired of saying it. He had said it so often before. "But it's easy to be drawn into things... That's why your mum would like to meet your friends. That's all we're saying."

Of course my mum had to back him up. "I have to know you're not getting in with the wrong crowd again, Logan."

The last thing I wanted was my friends meeting my mum. After all, they never asked me to come to their houses to meet their families. How stupid would I look to them?

"I'm not bringing my friends home for tea!"

Vince sat across from me. He leaned close, he even managed a smile. "Well, at least tell us who they are."

I didn't even bother to answer that. I was afraid to tell them, afraid Vince would check them out and the boys would find out and then they would never want me as a friend again. And I wouldn't blame them.

I'd had enough of my mum and Vince. It would only get worse if I stayed in. Without another word, I slammed my way out of the house. I heard my mum shouting after me, "Logan! Come back."

And then Vince saying, "Leave him be, Marie. Let him cool down. He'll come back."

I waited on the walkway for a few minutes, to see if she'd come after me. Waited, hoped, for the door to be hauled open and for her to come running out. She didn't. She never did.

Would I have gone back into the house if she had? I don't know, but I know what happened that night was the beginning of it all.

FOUR

I hammered along the walkway, could hear the anger in my footsteps. I took the wet stairs too quickly, lost my footing and slipped. I went right down with my back bouncing off every step. I let out a yell as I landed at the bottom. My butt ached, my back ached. I felt a hand on my shoulder.

I looked round quickly, sure it was Vince. He'd come after me to insist I come back home. I was ready for another argument.

But it wasn't Vince. It was Lucie.

Lucie is in my class at school. She lives nearby, in one of the other walk-up apartments. She has blonde hair that always looks as if she's cut it herself – I don't think she ever bothers combing it. That night she wore it almost up in a ponytail, but not quite. Half of it hung in spikes on her shoulders. She was another loner. Off the wall. 'A strange girl,' I heard some of the teachers say. I thought she was just different, and I kind of liked her for that. She sat down on the stairs beside me, offered me some of the gum she was always chewing.

"You hurt yourself?" she asked.

"No, I always come down the stairs on my back."

She gave me a punch. "You think you are 'all that'." She sketched the inverted commas with her fingers and giggled. "As the girly girls say!" One thing Lucie could never be called: a girly girl. She sniffed. "Had a fight?"

"As usual," I said.

"Bad thing, aggression," she said, as if she was an expert. "Better being laid back about things."

"If you were any more laid back you'd be horizontal," I laughed. And it was true. She never seemed to get upset about anything. Her mum and dad weren't really her mum and dad, but she'd been fostered by them since she was ten. They were better than a real mum and dad, she always said. I didn't know what had happened to her before, and she never talked about it, but I knew it was bad. It was so clear she loved this new family she had, and they loved her.

"Want to go for a coke?" she asked suddenly.

I liked Lucie. She never said or did anything you expected. It would have been nice to go for a coke with her and just sit somewhere and talk. I could talk to Lucie better than I could talk to anyone, even Baz. But just then I saw him. Baz. He stepped out from behind the flats, almost on cue, as if he'd known I was thinking about him. Lucie followed my eyes. "Why don't you just come with me?"

I stood up. "Another time, Lucie."

"I might not ask again," she called after me as I hurried off towards Baz.

FIVE

When I met up with Baz he stared back to where Lucie still sat. "That's that Lucie, isn't it? Why are you talking to her? You keep well back from her. Stick around with Lucie and they'll begin to think you're as weird as she is."

He always made it clear he didn't like her. I never asked him why. Part of me didn't want to know.

"She's really ok," I said.

"You think everybody's ok, mate." Baz's frown was gone; he was laughing again.

When we got to the precinct the boys were waiting for us.

"What's going on?" I asked.

Gary shrugged. "We were thinking about going to the

community centre." He said it quietly. He didn't look at Baz, almost as if he knew what he would say.

Baz didn't disappoint him. "Oh, that sounds like an exciting night out," he sneered.

Claude was swearing like a trooper. "Heard some of the boys saying it was good there. You can play snooker, and there's music..."

"And lashings and lashings of ginger beer?" Baz smirked. I thought it was funny because I had just said that to my mum, and I hadn't expected Baz would have even heard of the Famous Five.

Claude looked baffled. He'd obviously never read Enid Blyton. "Aye, I think there's ginger beer as well."

That made us all laugh, but it was clear Baz wasn't interested in going to any community centre.

I thought it sounded ok, but I wouldn't go against Baz. Mickey came along then, with his mutt on a lead, and Gary said to him. "Have you heard anything about the community centre, Mickey?"

To my surprise he shook his head, "Don't want to go there. Can't anyway. Out of bounds for us."

"Out of bounds?" I asked.

He looked around us all. "You wouldn't know, Logan, but the rest of you do. We'd have to go through Young Bow territory. They decide who gets in there and who doesn't."

"I forgot about the Young Bow," Gary said.

"Young Bow territory?"

"You must have seen the graffiti?" Gary said.

And I vaguely remembered it. Scrawled across the bridges over the dual carriageway, or on walls where we walked to Tesco. I'd even seen it from the motorway driving with Mum and Vince.

YOUNG BOW RULES

"You scared of them?" It was Baz who asked. "Scared of a bunch of numbnuts who call themselves the..." he stifled a giggle, "the Young Bow? Aw, come on."

"I'm not scared of anybody," Gary said. "But I'm not daft enough to go looking for trouble."

"Me neither," Claude agreed.

Ricky whined as if he was agreeing with them too.

"How are they gonny see us?" Baz wasn't about to let this go. For him, now, going to the community centre was a challenge. "A quick dash over the bridge across the dual carriageway, and we're there."

Gary shook his head. "A quick dash and a quick death. Not for me, pal."

"Never took you for a coward, Gary."

As soon as Baz said it, Gary leapt to his feet. I thought there could be a real fight. I stepped in between them. Held Gary back. "You're no coward, Gary. And you're right, no point looking for trouble. But this is a free country. We should be able to go where we want. I mean, a no-go area, here in Glasgow." I took a step back, looked around them. "It's a free country. That's all I'm saying."

I could tell Baz was pleased with me. I had diplomatic skills, he was always telling me. They came in handy with Baz.

"I double dare you!" he said, a big grin on his face. "Come on, we were just saying nothing ever happens here. Well, let's make something happen."

Everyone stopped talking. My heart was thumping. I was thinking fast. What would be the harm in just going to a community centre we had every right to visit?

"Well, I'm not going. Ricky wouldn't like it." In answer, as if he agreed with Mickey, Ricky let out a solitary bark.

"You sure you ain't a ventriloquist, Mickey?" Baz asked. "You got that mutt well trained."

It broke the tension, made us laugh. I felt relieved. I wondered if any of the others felt the same.

Only Baz seemed disappointed. "Take him home, Mickey. Just for tonight. Let's go somewhere without the dog for once. Let's do it."

I wanted to say, *No, let's not get involved.* If this Young Bow were as bad as Gary and the others said, there could be trouble. I wanted to do what my mum had been asking me to do. *Let's stay out of it.* That's what I wanted to say. But how could I go against Baz? And anyway, he was right. We weren't doing anything wrong. We wanted to go to the community centre. What was wrong with that? So instead I drew myself up as if I, too, was scared of nothing. I grinned. "Well, we're always saying there's nothing to do around here. So why don't we make something to do?"

I glanced at Baz. He was grinning back with those bright white teeth. Pleased with me.

SIX

We waited at the precinct for Mickey to come back minus Ricky, then we headed to the bridge that would take us to the other side of the motorway, and the community centre. It was a warm summer night, the kind of night people in Glasgow make the most of. There were lots of people about. Couples out on dates. Mums and dads out strolling with their children. Boys on bikes, racing dangerously, young men standing on corners in open-necked shirts with the sleeves rolled up well past the elbow, showing off their muscles.

We were just a group of boys heading for the community centre. No one was to know how nervous we were feeling about it. And we wouldn't have been doing it if it hadn't been for Baz.

"Just promise me, one sign of trouble and we run. Ok?" Mickey had said as soon as he came back, as if he'd been thinking about it all the way. He shrugged. "I don't care if anybody calls me a coward for saying that."

"I'm with you, Mickey," I told him as we began walking. "I'll be out of there faster than a speeding bullet." I looked at the boys. "What do this Young Bow crowd look like anyway?"

"You'll know them when you see them," Gary said. "Their leader calls himself Fury."

"Fury?" Baz laughed. "What does he think he is?"

Claude said, "I think that might be his real name. Sandy Fury." That set us all off laughing.

The further we walked, the more relaxed we became. The estate wasn't all tower blocks and run-down flats. It began to open up to newly built houses with gardens and garages. Gary pointed that out with pride, "They're always trying to improve this place, I mean look at that park." In the park people were walking their dogs, there were boys playing football, toddlers running around giggling while their parents sat on the grass watching them. It was such a peaceful summer evening I was suddenly sure nothing would happen. It was too nice a night for any trouble, and there was still no sign of this gang.

I fell into step beside Gary. "How did you hear about this community centre, Gary?"

"Couple of the girls in my class go there, said it was good fun."

Claude, walking ahead of us, turned round and giggled. "Walk in there and that's the last we'll see of Gary." He put on a girly voice. "Gary, Gary, I love you. Gary, Gary, will you be my boyfriend?"

That made us all laugh. All except Gary. "I'm not going there looking for girls," he said.

We were still laughing as we crossed the bridge. There was no sign of anyone barring our way, and I thought, with some relief, *They're not going to appear.*

We were almost at the other side, we had almost made it, when a crowd of boys stepped into view. It was as if they had been waiting for us, as if they had been guarding the bridge just to keep us out.

Gary had been right. I knew them as soon as I saw them. Wasn't rocket science to see they all belonged to the same gang, the Young Bow. My first thought was they looked daft. They were all dressed the same; they all looked the same. Hair slicked up with gel, all dressed in black, studded leather jackets, they looked as if they were copying something they'd seen on TV or in a film. I saw Baz put his hand over his mouth to stop himself from laughing out loud. But he was the only one who saw the funny side. We all stopped. I heard Mickey mutter under his breath, "Aw, naw."

The leader (why is it you can always tell which one is the leader?) moved to the front. He had an earring pierced into his eyebrow. This was Sandy Fury? He drew himself up to look taller than he was. He still wasn't as tall as Baz, I noticed.

"What's all this then?" his eyes scanned us, rested on Mickey. "Oh, look who it is. Where's the pet ferret the night?" His friends all seemed to find this hilarious. "Ricky, isn't it? Or, are you Mickey? I never know which one's the dug." His gang found this hilarious too.

I could sense Mickey beside me, his whole body tensing. But he said nothing.

Made bold by our silence, the boy took another step forward. "So, where do you think you're going?" He didn't wait for an answer. "Community centre's out of bounds to you lot."

Almost unnoticed, Mickey had taken a step back, so had Claude. Me and Gary held our place. It was Baz who spoke for us. "Says who?" He didn't sound the least bit afraid, and I was shaking in my trainers. How could he sound so sure of himself, when I was so scared? I wished I could be like him.

"I know you... I've heard about you." The leader boy pointed a finger at Baz. "You're a nutjob."

The words were hardly out of his mouth when Baz ran at him. Fury hadn't expected that. Baz took him completely by surprise. Took them all by surprise. They stood still as statues for a second. Baz leapt on the boy and they both tumbled back onto the ground. I could see the other boys in the gang were ready to jump in. I shouted, "Come on!" We couldn't let Baz fight on his own. The boys didn't let me down. They ran and we all fell on them, like Predators on Aliens. I felt someone punch my eye, then my face. But I got in a good few punches myself. I wasn't a fighter, but in Aberdeen I had learned to hold my own. I was vaguely aware of a crowd gathering at the Young Bow side of the bridge, and I heard someone yell, urging us to stop. I even spotted some on their phones taking videos of us. I didn't even know which one of the Young Bow I was fighting with. We were all tangled up, arms and legs and kicks and punches.

Then, in the distance, I could hear the police siren.

"Noo, you're for it!" said someone in the crowd.

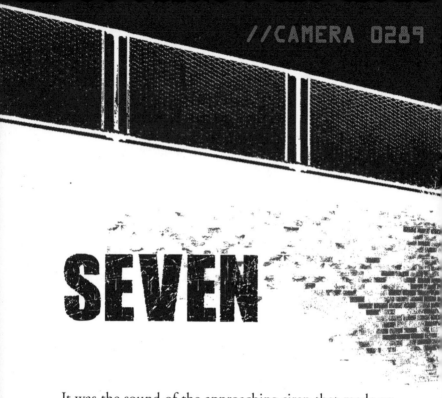

SEVEN

It was the sound of the approaching siren that made us get to our feet, still fighting and throwing punches, but at the same time pushing each other away. That siren was coming closer. The Young Bow stepped back. The leader pointed at me, then his finger moved round us all. "This isn't finished, pal. Watch out, we'll be coming after you lot."

People were standing around, shaking their heads, watching us. I only realised then that my mouth was bleeding. I wiped it off with the back of my hand and looked about. A police car screeched to a halt on the walkway back on our side of the bridge. The Young Bow saw it too. They were off their mark quick. But I could

36

see another police car on their side, cutting off their escape. I knew they wouldn't get very far.

Mickey was hoofing it back across the bridge. I'd never seen him run so fast, and Baz had disappeared too. I grabbed at Gary, "Come on!" We both began to run. But we didn't make it. By the time we got across, two policemen were waiting for us. They were already holding Claude by the arms.

"It wasn't our fault!" Gary shouted as he ran toward them. He was pointing back at the Young Bow. "We were only going to the community centre, they wouldn't let us past."

"*They* were fighting with *us*," I said. "It's them you should be arresting."

One of the cops held up his hand. "We're not arresting you." He even managed a hint of a smile. "But you can't fight like that – absolutely not in a public place. You're lucky we had cars cruising the area when the call came in." He was talking as if we would have been beaten to a pulp if they hadn't turned up.

I wasn't having that. "We could have handled them," I said.

He raised an eyebrow as if he doubted it. Then he said, "Don't worry, you're not in any real trouble."

Claude, Gary and I were bundled into the back of the police car.

"Where are you taking us?" I asked, though I knew the answer. They were taking us all home. Just what

I needed: my mum seeing me brought back by the police.

Gary was really annoyed. "Aw naw, do my mum and dad have to know? I never did anything wrong. It wasn't our fault." How many times did we have to tell them?

One of the policemen turned round to us. "We'll make sure your parents know that."

It was the first time I'd seen where the other boys lived. I hadn't gotten to know much of the estate, still couldn't find my way around it, and I'd seen nothing of Glasgow. Gary lived in a cosy-looking house in a neat line of terraces. His garden was filled with flowers, and there was a wooden bench beneath the front window. His mother was out of the door and running down the path as soon as the police car drew up. Right away I could see where Gary got his looks from. His mum was really good looking, and she had copper-red hair that seemed to flame in the light from the setting sun. "What happened to my boy?" she shouted, and as he came out of the car, she grabbed him and clutched him close against her. Gary's face went red when she did that.

"I never did anything wrong, Mum," he mumbled.

The older policeman said nothing, he only followed Gary and his mum up the path and inside the house. Claude and I didn't say a word while we waited. I think we were both a bit scared. The policeman who was left in the car with us was younger. He said, "You know, sometimes just arriving home in a police car is enough to put you off a life of crime. That's what we hope anyway."

"A life of crime? We were the ones who were attacked!" I told him again.

Claude leaned forward, covering his face with his hands. "My maw is going to kill me."

"Ah well," the policeman said. "If she does, that *is* a custodial offence. You tell her that before you croak it." He obviously thought he was a bit of a comedian, hoped that his light-hearted tone would make us feel better. It didn't.

Gary's mum had already phoned Claude's mum, so she was prepared for our arrival. By the time we got to his house – one of the newest on the estate, still all spick and span – she was waiting at the gate and when the car came to a halt she didn't look as if she was going to kill Claude, it was the policemen I thought she was about to attack.

She was a ball of fat that shook like a jelly as she pulled open the gate and ran towards the car. "These boys were only protecting themselves; you should be doing something about these blinking gangs – stopping decent boys from going to the community centre! And what do you lot do? *You* arrest *them*! Away and solve a murder! We get plenty of them here as well. It's my tax money that's paying for you lot, and this is the thanks we get." Now I could see where Claude learned so many of his swear words. All through this tirade Claude's mum was swearing like the offshore men I used to hear in Aberdeen.

This time neither of the policemen went inside the house. I think they were scared of her actually, and I didn't blame them. They went as far as the front door, stood there until it was slammed in their faces, and then they turned and got back into the car.

"Ha, wouldn't like to bring home a broken pay packet to that one," the comedian said. The other one laughed. I didn't quite know what he was talking about.

As we drove to my house, I wondered what my mother would say. Would she hug me like Gary's mum, or bawl at the cops like Claude's?

I could feel my mood changing the closer we got to the flat. I could feel my anger growing too. We had done nothing wrong. We had every right to go to the community centre. And yet, I was the one who was going to get into trouble. Taken home in a police car for all the world to see, as if I was some common criminal. It wasn't fair. Nothing was fair. My life wasn't fair.

What did I have? I had no dad. My mother thought more of her new boyfriend than she did of me. I had been taken away from the friends I had in Aberdeen, and dumped here. I was trying my best to stay out of trouble. None of what had happened had been my fault.

I was slumped in the back of the car. The older policeman must have seen by my face how down I was. "Don't worry, son. We'll make sure your mum knows you're not in any real trouble. It'll be fine."

EIGHT

"Have you got to come in with me?" I asked the policeman. "I'd rather go in on my own."

He leaned over the back of the seat. "Sorry, son. As I told you, you're not in any real trouble, but we have to make sure your parents know what's happened and the trouble you might have gotten into."

"Parent," I said. "I've only got one. I don't have a dad."

He nodded. "Oh. Sorry."

"My mum's got a boyfriend though." I made sure he knew that. I wanted him, both of them, to know that crew-cut Vince of the tattoos, ex-SAS, was no dad of mine.

In fact, it was Vince who opened the door. He

looked from the policemen to me, and you could see his annoyance written all over his face. He'd never make a poker player. Everything about him said, 'What's he done now?'

"Are you Mr Massie?" the older policeman asked.

I turned on him. "I told you. I don't have a dad. He's not my dad."

"Do you want to speak to my wife?"

"Your wife?"

Vince nodded. I never let anyone know they were married. Kept hoping it wasn't true. "Yes, my wife. He didn't tell you that we were married, I suppose. Come on in."

My mum came running down the hall then. "What's happened?"

The policeman held up his hands. "The boy's not in any trouble. Him and his friends were heading for the community centre and they were confronted by one of the gangs in the area. They were protecting themselves. It turned into a fight."

It was then I remembered Baz had been the first one to jump in. I hoped they never found that out. Of course I didn't mention that Baz or Mickey had been there too. I knew none of the boys would. It would have been a betrayal even to name them.

As the policeman spoke, my mum was leading both of them into the living room. "I always warn him to stay out of trouble." She glanced at Vince when she said that, and I could tell they'd been talking about me. Well, I had lived down to all their expectations, hadn't I? Here I was, escorted home by the police.

"Better keeping clear of these gangs." This was Vince. "We keep telling him that."

"We were trying to go to the community centre. That was all. But this gang, the Young Bow—" I felt I spat the words out, "—that's in their territory, and they decide who gets in and who doesn't. They were barring our way. Have you ever heard anything so stupid?"

The younger policeman said, "You can get to the community centre, you know. They send a bus to the precinct, takes you there and takes you back."

Couldn't they understand this is what really annoyed me? "And that's what we should do then? Get a bus, like a bunch of wee scaredy-cat boys, so we don't give the Young Bow any bother?"

"Logan!" My mum sounded exasperated. "The policeman's trying to be helpful."

"This is supposed to be a free country." I nodded across to Vince. "Is that not what Rambo here was fighting for?"

I could see I was losing any sympathy I'd had from the two policemen. I was turning into a boy with a bad attitude. I didn't care. We hadn't done anything bad. We should be able to go anywhere we wanted. What was I saying that was so wrong?

After that, I said nothing. It was all very civilised till

the police left and then it was Vince who gave me the lecture, not my mum. This was the man who'd been chucked out of the army, now he couldn't get a job. My mum was the sole wage-earner, and she didn't exactly get executive pay at the call centre. He was living off her, he should be grateful. Instead, he went on about how they had warned me about gangs and fighting and stuff like that, while my mum sat on the sofa, looking as if she was ready to cry again.

"All we asked you to do was to stay away from trouble. And you couldn't even do that, could you? Do you do this deliberately to upset your mum?"

What was it to do with him? I wanted to know. It's my mum's house, not his. It's in her name, I was sure of it. Why didn't she throw him out?

And do you know what he said? "You live in another world, Logan."

"I didn't do anything wrong!" I had said it over and over, and still he didn't listen. "And it's not your house," I reminded him again.

He didn't like that. My mum stepped in between us. I wondered if she thought he was going to hit me. Though he never has. Got to admit that. Never even come near it. If he'd ever lifted his hand to me, he's the one who would have been in trouble.

"You promised me, Logan." Her voice was breaking, as if her throat hurt, as if she had been crying for a long time. Long before tonight.

45

But her tears couldn't get to me any more. Her boyfriend was the only one who mattered to her. I didn't. Do you know how that makes you feel? If only my dad was here. Why did he have to die!

Die!

There, I'd said it. I'd said the word, though it broke my heart. He had died and left me. Everybody deserts me, that's how I felt. That was the excuse for everything I did.

I ran out of the house and banged the door and stood on the walkway and yelled – like some kind of ancient warrior. My voice seemed to bounce off the walls and then it rose up through the canyons of the high-rise flats and into the night.

Doors opened on the balcony, neighbours took one look at me and shut them again. None of them liked me, I was sure of it. They'd probably seen me being escorted home by the cops, thought I'd done something terrible. They all thought I was trouble, though I'd never done anything to them.

"There's something wrong with that Logan boy," I'd heard one of them whisper as I passed their door. How they'd come to that conclusion I don't know – I'd never done anything to them. *Stuff them*, I thought. *Why should I care what they think?*

And then Vince comes running out of the flat. "What on earth do you think you're playing at?!"

I pushed past him and slammed back inside. If he was

going to apologise to the neighbours, he could do it by himself.

I heard him and Mum talking about me as I lay in my bed. Tried not to listen but the walls are like paper, you could hear the whisper of a whisper through them.

"Out of control," I heard Vince say. "You really have to do something about him, Marie."

I waited for her answer, waited to hear her shout, tell him to get out of her house: *My son comes first!* But there was no answer. I could only hear muffled voices, and then there was silence. She was probably whispering sweet nothings in his tattooed ear.

NINE

I saw Baz next day. He was waiting for me at the corner when I was heading for the precinct. "Where did you go to last night?" I asked him.

He laughed. "I hoofed it. What was the point of me hanging about? No point in all of us getting lifted."

I told him about being taken home by the police. "You should have heard what I got when I got back."

He laughed, another of his big belly laughs. "I did actually. You were yelling that loud I could have heard you in Aberdeen."

I laughed too. He always made me feel better.

The boys were all at the precinct. All with a tale to tell. A big warning for Gary from his dad, who didn't like any contact with the law. As for Claude's mum, she had spoiled him rotten, sent out for a deep-fried pizza and chips to make him feel better. I told them what happened to me, and there were nods of sympathy, until Gary said, "I thought you'd be used to the police taking you home."

I'd told them once, in a stupid moment, about things that had happened in Aberdeen when I was running with a bad crowd. I'd been trying to show off to them, show them how tough I was. It annoyed me now that Gary brought that up.

"Things have been different here though, haven't they?" Baz said it, his tone daring Gary to challenge it.

But Gary did. "Not last night they weren't!" Then he held up his hands as if he was surrendering. "Sorry, Logan, shouldn't have said that."

I patted him on the back. He didn't often talk back to Baz. That took a bit of nerve, and I liked Gary, I liked how he always stuck up for his dad. Didn't matter if his old man was a bit of a crook, or that there were times when he had lost his temper with Gary and lifted his hand to him. He thought his dad was brilliant in spite of everything.

I turned to Mickey. He was sitting on the pavement, his mangy dog curled up by his feet. "What about you, Mickey? You did a runner last night."

He shook his head. "I would have got hell if I'd been picked up by the cops. My dad would have killed me or worse, even if he knew it wasn't my fault."

Nobody, I noticed, asked why Baz had run off. And Baz didn't offer any explanation either.

"I don't know what we were even thinking about, going there," Claude said. "Bad idea."

"We did it, because we stand for freedom!" I got to my feet and yelled: "FREEDOM!"

Claude laughed. "Well said, Logan."

"But who says we'll not do it again, eh? It's too dangerous," Mickey asked.

"Oh, come on," said Baz. "What was dangerous? We got in a fight, proved we could stand up to that gang. Gave them a good run for their money, didn't we?"

"I think we were just lucky the cops came when they did," said Mickey.

He was right, I probably knew that, but there had been something exciting about confronting the Young Bow, one of the worst gangs in the area, and standing up to them. I had been scared, but excited too. I wanted to have that feeling again, the feeling I had had last night.

"They said it wasn't finished. They're gonny get us back," Gary said.

I shrugged. "Well, we let them see we're not scared of them. If they want to mess with us, let them try."

TEN

I didn't go out for the next couple of nights. My mum was so pleased about that. She had a couple of days off and we spent them together, just her and me. The atmosphere in the house was so much better. Even with Vince – he was smiling, whistling. And Mum and I had real talks, not arguments. This was a new start for us here in Glasgow, she said. Things were going to be good from now on. She was waiting for news about a house well away from here. My heart fell when she said that. A new beginning, moving to a new area, just when I was making friends here. I would lose Baz, and the rest of the boys. She didn't understand how hard it was for me to make new friends, to begin again somewhere different.

I didn't say any of that to her, of course. I didn't want to make my mother unhappy. It just seemed I never got the chance to fit in anywhere. And no matter how hard I tried, things went wrong.

She'd made all my favourite teas, mince and potatoes, macaroni cheese, and we ate together, and, you know, just being together, without Vince, it was almost like old times. I could almost imagine us waiting for my dad to come in, then Mum putting out his tea, and the three of us sitting round the table while he told us all about his day. Only we weren't waiting for Dad any more, were we? It was Vince we waited for now.

So don't think I didn't consider staying in. Staying in for the rest of my life. But I was a boy. I couldn't stay in forever.

Mum went back to work. She was working a night shift, and Vince was out, but he would be coming in later and I couldn't stand the thought of sitting in with just him. I could be out and back, and Mum need never know. What could possibly go wrong with that? So I left the house after she had gone to work, to go and meet up with the boys.

I was just running through the park towards the precinct, when I heard the voice. "You out the other night?"

The grass here was overgrown, the swings were broken. I didn't see anyone at first. Then, in one of those eerie moments that sends a shiver down your spine, Lucie stepped out of nowhere. She had a habit of doing that. You wouldn't hear her coming, or see her anywhere, and suddenly, there she'd be. Scared the life out of people sometimes.

I looked around. Not a soul in sight. She was completely alone. Yet, Lucie never seemed to be afraid to be alone. For other people, especially here, the opposite was true. In fact she was the one people stayed back from. People were afraid of her. Not that she was a bully, or a girl who started fights. It was just that she was strange.

"Her lift doesn't go to the top floor," I'd heard someone say.

So, there was something wrong with me, and her lift didn't go to the top floor. We were well matched, Lucie and me.

She even looked weird. I had to admit it. She looked like no other girl I had ever met. She had attempted once again to put her hair in a ponytail, hadn't quite succeeded. Half of it stuck out in spiky strands. The streetlamp gave her face an orange glow. She was bouncing a football on the ground. She was a good football player, was Lucie. A lot better than I was. She asked again, "Were you? The other night? Out?"

I answered her question with one of my own. "Were you?"

"Me? Joking? I've not got any friends, remember? Was it you I saw getting a personal escort home?" She laughed.

"What makes you think that was me?"

She plonked herself down on the lopsided roundabout, caught the ball and held it on her knee. "It's hard to miss somebody your size in the middle of two big cops. Were you in handcuffs?"

"I wasn't being arrested. I hadn't done anything wrong." And before I could stop myself I was telling her all about the Young Bow and what had happened that night. "I didn't even really want to go to the community centre."

"So why did you?"

I just shrugged. Couldn't tell her it was all down to Baz.

She shook her head and her ponytail completely escaped. I imagined her hair falling in long golden strands on her shoulders. It didn't. It still stuck out in spikes. "You got to do everything everybody else does? You're easily led, do you know that? Stay out of trouble, why don't you?"

"What's it to you?" She was talking like my mum.

"Nothing. But you're on a final warning, aren't you? You don't want to get into any more trouble, Logan. I like you." Honesty was another thing that made Lucie different. "Don't like many people, Logan. Do you like me?" she asked suddenly.

"If I say yes, does that mean we're engaged, Lucie?"

That made her laugh again. "You should be so lucky."

The truth was, I did like her. I liked walking to school

54

with her, talking with her. I could say things to Lucie. And I did listen to her. For all she was a bit off the wall, she talked a lot of sense.

"You going out again? Not across the bridge, I hope. They'll be waiting for you."

"No. Not across the bridge. We'll stay away from the Young Bow from now on."

I looked across the park. Baz was there, his hands thrust deep into the pockets of his hoodie, waiting for me. I held my hands up in a wave.

Lucie followed my gaze. She ignored him. "Want a kick about?"

"I've got to go, Lucie."

She aimed a long hard kick in Baz's direction. If she expected him to kick the ball back she had another thing coming. Baz just stood there, glaring at her, letting the ball dribble to a stop at his feet. It was me who picked it up when I ran toward him. I threw it back to Lucie. "Another time, I promise."

She caught the ball and yelled back, "You're weirder than me."

And I don't know who she was speaking to – me or Baz.

ELEVEN

"I keep telling you. You shouldn't have anything to do with her," Baz said as we ran. "She's not right in the head."

He had never liked her. Just as she didn't like him. I didn't want to remind him that I did like her. And she was in my class at school – hard to ignore her. So I said nothing. I said nothing because I was always afraid to annoy Baz. I can see that now.

There was no time to talk about Lucie anyway. There were other things on our minds.

We caught up with the rest of the boys at the precinct. "So where to tonight, boys?" Baz called to them.

"It's a nice night, 'mon we'll go for a walk," Gary suggested.

"Opposite direction from the bridge," Claude said.

"I second that," said Mickey, and Ricky barked with approval.

Baz was more annoyed than the rest of us that there were areas out of bounds. "Why should that be? This is a free country, ain't it?"

Gary shrugged. "It's just the way it is around here. Boys from the Drago in my class, they won't even sit in the same group as the Gardy Boys."

Baz snorted.

"Drago?" I asked. "Gardy Boys? Where do they get these names?"

"Maybe they didn't have enough spray left in their cans for the 'n'. They really wanted to be called 'the Dragons'."

Gary laughed. "Sometimes you say the craziest things, Logan."

"These gangs get better by the minute."

"Nothing funny about them though," Claude said. "Dragos are nearly as bad as the Young Bow."

"But not quite," Mickey said. "Nobody's as bad as the Young Bow."

"Anybody for getting that bus... the one that takes us to the community centre?" Gary said it warily, his eyes darting around to check out what people thought. It was Baz who answered him.

"I can just imagine us sitting on the bus, and passing that bunch we had the fight with. That would really give them a laugh, eh? 'Ooo, there's them wee boys on the bus.'"

I had to admit he was right about that. We would just look stupid. Finally, the other boys agreed.

"There must be some place we can go."

"There's a few other gangs we've got to avoid."

Baz kicked the wall. "Aw, come on. More no-go areas."

Mickey laughed. "No, we're safe here. This is Drago territory. Arch enemies of the Young Bow. Young Bow would never risk coming in here."

"This town ain't big enough for both of us." Baz had us laughing with his American accent.

"There really is nothing to do in this dump," Claude moaned.

"We could go swimming. There's a good swimming pool here," Gary suggested. "And I don't think this place is a dump. It's getting better. All these new houses being built. This is a great estate. The people are terrific. They stick by each other, they're kind." That was something I really liked about Gary. He always saw the best in people. While I looked at the gutter, he saw only stars.

Baz didn't laugh. "Swimming?" he sneered, as if Gary had suggested ballet dancing. I wondered then if maybe Baz couldn't swim, and he didn't want to tell us. I wouldn't have blamed him. I couldn't swim either, the doggy paddle was the best I could do. I'd be mortified if the rest of them had wanted to go swimming. But a moment later it seemed I was wrong about Baz.

"I used to swim all the time. Used to love it," Baz went on. "Diving, got medals as well." I'd never known that. "But here," and now he sneered again. "Bunch of amateurs here. Weans splashing about. Old men farting in the water."

"Maybe if you had your own private pool it would be different, eh?" Gary said, and I wondered was he being sarcastic?

"I will one day," Baz said. He said it as if he meant it.

Just then, a boy I didn't recognise came hurrying up to us. "Hi Gary, Mickey..."

"What's up, Tadge?"

"You lot better be careful. Word on the street is the Young Bow are looking for you." He included us all in the 'you'. "You better watch your backs."

We were all alert in a second. "Tonight?"

Tadge nodded.

"Are they coming here?"

He nodded again.

"How come they can come here, but we can't go there?" I asked.

"This is rubbish!" Baz spat on the ground.

This Tadge looked around, almost as if he expected the Young Bow to suddenly rush from between the shops, armed and ready for battle. "Just watch yourself, Gary. If I hear anything, I'll let you know."

"They said they'd get us," Gary said. "And now they're coming. What do we do?"

"Run!" Claude said. He would have been off if Gary hadn't held him back.

"I'm going home." Mickey was always the first to leave the sinking ship. Him and his dog.

Baz stood up. "So, we just hide in our houses till they go away?"

Mickey only thought about it for a moment. "Sounds like a good idea to me."

"And tomorrow night... if they come back? What do we do then?"

Even Gary saw the sense in that. "They're going to just keep coming back."

"I'm not going to fight with the Young Bow," Claude was shaking his head. "Once was enough for me. We don't do fighting."

"None of us wants a fight with them," I agreed.

They were coming to get us. I imagined them, like the villains in an old cowboy movie, a line of them heading our way.

"So tell me, smart alec. What do we do? Face up to them, fight them, get taken home again in a cop car? Or... run back home and hide under the bed?"

"We should never have gone there the other night," Claude said.

"And if we hide, we'll get a reputation. Cowards." This was Gary.

I shook my head. "There has to be another way, something else we could do."

It seemed we were trapped. No matter what we did, we were done for.

We were all silent for a moment, trying to think up a way out of this that wouldn't involve blood being shed. Our blood.

Baz stood up, a big smile spread across his face. He snapped his fingers. "I think I might have an idea. And if it works... our troubles will be over."

TWELVE

We had all listened to Baz's idea, our mouths hanging open – at least that was the way I imagined it. What he was suggesting was dangerous, and could end up getting us into even more trouble. But he was right, if it worked...

So here we were, doing exactly as he wanted us to do. We had talked about it, discussed it, argued about it and finally decided to just go for it. Or had Baz decided for us? I'm still not sure.

We had to ask this Tadge to help us. He had come out of the takeaway and Gary had called him over. Told him what we needed him to do. He was up for it, but only if Gary would put in a good word for him with a girl in their class. Then we had waited at the shops for Mickey while he ran home with his dog. To be honest, none of us had been sure if he would ever come back.

But he did. He looked nervous and he was shouting as he ran towards us, "They're heading here. A couple of boys told me. Does Tadge know what he's got to do?"

Gary held up his phone. "He's just texted me. He's done it."

Mickey was looking back as if he expected the Young Bow to be running at his heels. "We've got to move."

Baz held us his hands. "Right, we know exactly what we're doing?" He looked around at us. We all nodded.

It was Gary who had decided where we should go. He knew the estate better than anybody. "We know where we're heading, don't we?" His phone buzzed then. He checked it. "That's Tadge just texted me again. The Young Bow are crossing the bridge."

My heart drummed in my chest. "Ok, let's go."

We didn't run. I think I remember that more than anything. Now that we had a plan, we moved confidently. I can picture it in my mind still, and I love how we walked, a line of us, like... like the Magnificent Seven. Ever seen that movie? Ok, there weren't seven of us, but the feeling was the same.

My legs shook though. We weren't running away from the Young Bow. We were heading straight for them. It was dangerous, and exciting at the same time. Gary was up there with Baz, they knew exactly where they were going. Me and Mickey and Claude followed behind.

We saw them in the distance, the Young Bow. I still thought they looked stupid. Trying to be so cool in black leather and studs, trying too hard. They stopped dead when they saw us.

"Heard we were coming, did you?" the leader, this guy Fury, shouted at us. His lip curled up in a sneer.

It was Baz who spoke for us. And what he said made my legs shake even more. "Is that you, Furry? Didn't recognise you under all that gel."

Fury's eyes went wild. "It's Fury! Fury!" he yelled at Baz.

Baz answered him, cool as could be. "I think Furry suits you better."

If I hadn't been so scared, I think I would have laughed.

Furry – can't call him anything else now – turned to his gang: "Get them!"

Before he had even finished saying it, we had turned and were running like crazy.

I heard one of them shout behind us, "Aye run, but we're going to get you anyway!"

We kept close, the five of us. We knew where we were going, at least Gary did. The Young Bow didn't.

"What if they catch us?" Claude whispered breathlessly. He could never run as fast as the rest of us.

"Then we fight," I told him. "If that's what we've got to do. We fight. We don't leave anybody. I promise."

And Baz agreed with me right away. He turned and yelled, "All for one..."

Gary finished for him, "And every man for himself."

So I ran with Claude, behind the rest. I had promised him I'd stay with him, and I wasn't going to let him down. Even when I could hear the Young Bow closing in, and Claude stumbled beside me, I didn't run on ahead.

We ran through streets, and up lanes, and climbed over walls, and finally burst into open ground where houses had been demolished and new builds would soon spring up. The Young Bow were close behind us, and the chase was only making them mad. "Turn and fight!" they were all yelling.

We didn't waste our breath answering them. I glanced at Claude, he was breathing heavy, his face bubbled with sweat. "You can make it, Claude," I whispered.

"We're nearly there," Gary shouted. Now we were back among canyons of tenements and lock-ups and warehouses. "Round the next corner. Up here."

He held up his hand and waved in the direction we were to go, and we all followed him. We found ourselves in an alley. There were lock-up garages on one side, and a big empty warehouse on the other. Signs plastered all over the walls and windows:

TO BUY OR LEASE

And in front of us, brick wall. We had run into a dead end.

Gary and Baz and Mickey were already there, standing in front of the brick wall, facing us.

"Good for you, Logan," Gary shouted, when he saw I had paced it with Claude. And even in that moment when I was so scared, I felt proud.

"Hey, we made it, Claude." I took his arm to help him on those last few steps.

When we reached the others, Claude stopped. He bent over, hands on his knees, trying to get his breath back. He glanced up at me and smiled. "Thanks, Logan. I'll not forget that."

We were all waiting, standing in a line, when the Young Bow came into view. Fury let out a yell of triumph, "Rats in a trap!" He pointed all round the alley. "You ran into a dead end. You idiots. Nowhere to run now, boys!"

They all laughed, Fury and his gang, sure there was nothing we could do.

We were trapped.

And then, as if they had all the time in the world, the Young Bow started walking up the alley towards us, one slow, menacing step at a time.

THIRTEEN

And at that moment, behind them, another group of boys arrived. Skidding round the corner into the alley, forming at once into a line and looking every bit as menacing as the Young Bow. The Dragos had come.

"Guess who's caught in a trap noo, Fury?" one of them called out.

Fury swung round. He looked at them and back to us, then back to them again. He was puzzled. They were all puzzled.

That had been the plan all along. Baz's brilliant plan. The Young Bow might have thought they were chasing us, but actually, we had been leading them. Leading them into an ambush.

Gary had told Tadge where we would run to, the dead end where the Dragos could find their archenemies, and Tadge had let the Dragos know our plan.

We didn't wait to see what happened next, though we heard about it later. Turned into a running battle through the streets of the estate. Baz was on the roof of one of the lock-ups as soon as Fury's back was turned, and then in the same moment Gary was up there too, jumping on a wooden crate that had been left lying about, helping each of us in turn. They were taller than the rest of us; Mickey, Claude and I could never have made it up there on our own. And then we were off, running over the roofs of the lock-ups, and leaping back down onto the ground, out of sight. As we ran we could hear yells and shouts in the distance. The fight had begun.

"That was brilliant!" Gary's face was red with excitement. "It worked."

"I didn't think it would," Mickey said. "I was sure they'd catch us."

"You were in front of everybody else, wee man," I told him. "I've never seen you run so fast."

"It's called terror. I've never been so scared."

We stopped for a moment to catch our breath. We couldn't stop laughing and going over it again and again. "Furry! Where did you come up with that one?"

Baz was laughing. "He'll never be called anything else from now on."

"Furry of the Young Bow!"

"Hey," Baz began to run again, and we all followed him. "I've got a great idea."

"Another one!" Claude shouted.

We followed him to one of the underpasses, where I had seen the graffiti earlier.

FURY AND THE
YOUNG BOW RULE

Baz picked up a piece of slate from the ground and began scraping it against the wall, using it to add one more letter.

"What are you doing?" Gary asked him.

Baz didn't answer. He stepped back when he was finished. And when we saw what he had scrawled, we all laughed.

FURY AND THE
YOUNG BOW RULE

He'll know that was you, Baz, I almost said. But I didn't. Our mood was so great. Was it adrenalin? We felt we had been clever and smart and I didn't want the feeling to end.

That night, for the first time, I really felt like one of the gang. Claude slapping me on the back, thanking me. Gary grinning at me. A grin that said I'd done good. I had a feeling of belonging I had never had before.

FOURTEEN

We kept running through alleys and underpasses, leaping from walls, seeing how high we could jump, still talking about the chase. We were all totally hyper.

We stumbled across a long line of cars parked outside some houses. All expensive-looking Mercs and BMWs and even a red Porsche. "Look at all these cars," Baz said. "Bet some of them are unlocked."

Gary agreed. "My dad says people always leave cars unlocked. You wouldn't believe how many."

Baz turned to him and laughed. "That how he gets all his cheap stuff, Gary, eh? Nicks it out of unlocked cars, does he?"

Gary's smile disappeared in an instant. He would have

flown at Baz, but Mickey held him back. "Hey, that's a bit much, pal," he said to Baz.

Baz knew he had said the wrong thing. He held up his hands. "Sorry, sorry, I open my big mouth and my foot flies right in."

He grinned at Gary, and finally Gary grinned back. I was so glad that, for once, Baz had apologised. This wonderful mood we had was too good to lose.

Mickey took a step closer to the Porsche. "Hey look at the trim in this one. It's real class." Claude came up beside him, and leaned against the car. All hell broke loose: the alarm began to sound, ricocheting around the street. Suddenly, a window was flung open, someone shouted, "What do you think you're playing at!"

And then a front door was pulled wide. A man came running out. Then another, then three. Hard men, and they were angry.

Gary held up his hands. "We were just looking!" he yelled.

"I'm not waiting to explain," Claude said.

Baz was off first. "Let's go!" he shouted. And we were right behind him.

And yet we were still laughing as we ran. It only added to our mood. We almost flew round corners, up flights of stairs, raced across streets, threw ourselves over walls, as if they were still on our tail, though they had given up the chase long ago.

So many areas here were just waste ground, with weeds springing up through cracks in the old pavements. Buildings demolished, waiting for new houses to be built in their place. There was not a soul to be seen. We were maybe only fifteen minutes from home, yet it was so deserted and silent, it felt like a million miles. It felt like another world. We were heading towards blocks that were still standing, but they all looked derelict and empty. The night was growing darker, heavy clouds covered the setting sun, the wind whipped up litter and leaves.

"Let's get out of here," Claude said. "This place is creepy. You could make a great horror movie here." He screwed his face up, trying to look scary. "You know – something coming out of these empty buildings, or something inside them… watching us…"

"Is that your horror face, Claude?" Baz shouted. "Wouldn't have known the difference."

Claude began running backwards, arms outstretched, face in horror mode, roaring at us.

He was so busy pretending to be some kind of monster that he back-stepped round a corner and fell over someone crouched on the ground. The guy fell back, so did Claude, and we were all running so fast behind him that we tumbled on top of both of them.

Claude jumped to his feet. "Sorry Mr—"

The guy lay back on the ground, looked up at us and grinned. One of his front teeth was missing and he had the bluest eyes I had ever seen. "Just come at the right time, boys. Need a hand here." He scrambled to his feet. "I'm trying to lift this." It was a roller-shutter door into what looked like an empty warehouse. "I think it's stuck."

Baz was the first one to step forward to help. He crouched beside the guy and tried to lift the door. It was still stuck.

Baz turned to us, puzzled, with a 'What are you just standing there for?' look on his face. "Come on boys, is nobody gonny help here?"

I glanced around. The street was deserted. There was a long line of boarded-up shops and premises on this block, some with derelict flats above them. Why was this guy going into this warehouse? It looked abandoned. And I decided he must work here, or he owns it. That's what I genuinely thought. Yet another voice was warning me to stay back. The guy's a junkie. You could tell by the greyness of his skin, and the black circles under his eyes.

"Come on then!" Baz said again.

I think it was the mood we were in. We'd tricked the Young Bow and now we were up for anything, wanting more. We all crouched down beside him and began hauling at the shutter door.

The guy grinned at us again, and I thought those oh-so-blue eyes of his had a coldness in them. With that tooth missing he reminded me of Long John Silver, you know that pirate out of *Treasure Island*? Kneeling there on the ground with this vacant smile on his face that didn't seem like a smile at all. What he said next made him sound even more like a pirate. "If you help me get in you can take a share in the loot."

The loot? What did he mean, *the loot?*

Gary got to his feet. He was shaking his head. "I know this guy. Al Butler," he whispered. "Bad news."

I stood up too, and looked all around, sure someone must be spying on us. But this one block seemed to be out of sight of everything. The sky was heavy and dark. The wind whipped past us again. It gave me a funny feeling. *We're not doing anything wrong,* I told myself, yet even at the time I remember thinking: *If we're doing nothing wrong, why do I feel guilty?*

FIFTEEN

We all helped in the end, even Gary, and we hauled and dragged at the edge of the steel till it bit into my fingers.

"Right, after three. Everybody pull together," this Al Butler said, and with one supreme effort we pulled. At last I could feel the steel rising, an inch at a time, until it suddenly flew from our hands and rolled to the top with a metallic clang. The noise made us all jump and look around, sure someone must have heard it. But no one came. There was no one to hear any sound.

Al Butler stepped inside the darkness of the warehouse and beckoned us to follow. None of us did. He swung round, spread out his arms, as if he was opening Ali Baba's treasure cave. I was almost waiting for him to say 'Abracadabra'. Instead he said, "Come on boys. One good turn deserves another." He took another step further inside and it was as if the gloom swallowed him up.

"I think we should just go," Gary said. But he didn't move.

"We could just go in for a look," Baz said, and I could see he really wanted to know what was inside. I did too.

"The place is derelict, what would be the harm in looking?" I didn't want to go against Baz, but I didn't want to annoy Gary either.

"There must be something in there, if he wants in so badly," Gary said. That just seemed to make Baz more determined.

"Oh come on. Who's for going in, just for a minute? Double dare you!" No one answered him. "Oh well, I'm going. I'm not scared."

"Me neither," Mickey said, and he was the bold one who stepped in after Al Butler. He turned back to us. "Aw come on, what's the harm?" And then he too disappeared into the gloom. It was as if they had gone through some black hole.

"Where are they going?" I asked. "Into the Twilight Zone?"

"Mickey?" Claude called out. There was no answer. Claude took a few steps inside. He called Mickey's name again, and still there was no answer. "Is anybody there?" he asked in a spooky voice. That made us giggle. And then out of the darkness, Mickey ran forward with a roar, his arms spread wide. Claude, taken completely by surprise, stepped back too quickly, and tumbled over a pile of boxes lying on the floor behind him.

Gary pulled at my arm. "We should just go," he said again. "I've heard of this guy. He's real trouble."

Why didn't we listen to him?

"Hey, we've had a really good night," Baz said. "We tricked the Young Bow, Gary. I might have come up with the idea, but you were the brains behind the rest. Don't tell me you're scared to go inside an old derelict warehouse. You're not, I know you're not, Gary." He pointed right at him. "You're scared of nothing."

He threw his words at him. It was a compliment, and it was a challenge too. I thought that was clever of Baz. It wouldn't have worked if he'd called Gary a coward, if he'd said he was too afraid to go inside. But to praise him, tell him he was scared of nothing – that was smart. And it worked.

Gary stood tall. "That's me. Your actual hero!" And with a whoop, he leapt inside, punching the air.

Me and Baz were the last ones in. Baz was usually first and I suppose I held back to go in beside him.

The warehouse was like a Tardis, it seemed so much bigger on the inside. It certainly wasn't empty. There were rolls of carpets and rugs piled up on the floor, and aisles of carpets all around, standing upright, like soldiers at attention.

"It's a carpet warehouse," Mickey said, disappointed.

Baz whipped out a rug lying in a pile. He flung it open. "You could pick up a nice wee something for your mammy," he said.

"Who does this place belong to?" I asked.

"Who cares?" Al Butler's voice came from somewhere between the carpets. I could hear him, but I couldn't see him.

"What do you mean?"

We must have all looked foolish then. His head popped up above a pile of rugs.

"Do you own this place?" Claude asked.

Al Butler didn't answer him. Instead he went again to the front door. "Here, help me get the shutters doon again. Don't want anybody spying on us."

Now was our chance to go. Why didn't we? But we didn't. Baz even helped him pull the shutters down.

I expected us to be plunged into darkness, but instead some kind of emergency lighting came on, and we were all bathed in an eerie red glow. It gave everything a surreal feel, as if we were caught up in some kind of weird dream. That's exactly how I felt. As if I was caught up in something unreal.

Mickey began walking around like a zombie, and in the dim red light he managed to look pretty scary. Claude immediately joined in. It was hard not to laugh at them. "No make-up required!" Gary said. And then it seemed we were all laughing, that nervous way, you know, when you're in a situation you've never been in before, and you don't know whether it's funny or serious. We all began walking about like zombies then.

We hardly noticed Al Butler, though I was vaguely aware he had gone into a room at the back. It sounded as if he was pulling out drawers, throwing things on the floor, not caring if anyone heard him – and how would they? There was no one anywhere nearby.

A few moments later he came swaggering down the aisle of carpet with a smug smile on his face. "Not bad, not bad," he was saying. He patted his pockets: they were bulging now. "Nice wee stash here," and he held up a wad of notes. "I always know where to look." He had a box in his other hand. "You can't leave empty-handed, boys. One good turn deserves another." He threw the box at Baz. "Here!"

Baz caught it deftly. "Hey, thanks." He actually said thanks! It was filled with Xbox games and Baz took them out and shoved them into my hands. "Stuff them in your pockets, we can sell them – come on. Who's going to miss them?"

I looked at Gary. He was shaking his head. And I knew he was right. We should just get out of here. I wanted to drop the games from my hand, but I felt as if they were glued there.

Everything seemed to be moving out of control. I began to be really afraid, and I couldn't think why. *Let's get out of here.* That's what I wanted to say. Why couldn't I say it?

SIXTEEN

Al Butler suddenly swung round. He looked up to a corner. "Aw naw, we've been spotted." He pointed, and we all followed his gaze. There was a camera in the corner, its one eye watching our every move. "Big Brother is watching you!"

Why didn't we run then? The CCTV camera scared me. We'd been seen. I could imagine that camera capturing us all looking up, our excitement turning to fear.

"Let's go," I said. I'm sure I was the one who said it.

Al Butler began to shout to the cameras. "Say hello to my boys!" He turned to us then, as if we were his best friends. "Don't worry about the cameras, boys." He held out his arms as if we should applaud him. "Destroy the cameras, and nobody sees us. Am I right? Of course I'm right."

"How are you going to destroy the cameras?" I asked him.

"Same way we're going to destroy everything else." His hands went deep into his hoodie and he brought out a yellow plastic bottle. I recognised it. It was stuff you use to light barbeques. We stood still, watching him, as he unscrewed the cap and began tipping it all over the carpets.

"What are you doing?" Claude asked. Yet we didn't need an answer. We knew what he was about to do. Al Butler took a box of matches from his pocket and opened it. He took out a match, a long match, and struck it, and a moment later a tiny flame appeared, pure yellow gold with flecks of green. I couldn't take my eyes from it, suspecting – knowing – what was going to happen next.

"You're not serious?" Baz asked.

Al Butler turned those ice-blue eyes on him. "We've been spotted. Only way to get rid of the cameras. We'll show them. Go up like a bonfire in here."

We all stood there for a moment, still like statues.

"No," I heard Gary behind me. That flame made him afraid too.

Al Butler waved the flame over the carpets, his eyes never leaving us. "It's up to you. What do you think?"

We were all silent. Mesmerised by the flame.

Baz broke the silence. His voice was a whisper. "I double dare you." I couldn't believe he'd said that.

Don't do it! I wanted to shout. Couldn't say a word. Al Butler wouldn't have listened anyway. Nothing would have stopped him. He'd come here prepared for this, with his lighter fuel and his long matches. Fire had always been his intention. He dropped the match to the carpet and a moment later he lit another, then another, and they all fell like little torches. The flames flickered for just a second – they seemed to reach out tiny tongues of fire, searching around for something to taste. For a moment I thought they would die. And then in a split second they touched the fuel and it was as if they became one and a monster opened its fiery mouth. In seconds the flames spread, sending tongues of orange and red and white leaping from one carpet to another. It had been a hot summer – everything was dry, dry as dust. It would go up quickly. I knew this in the moments the fire took hold, yet I still couldn't move. None of us could.

I had never seen a fire move so fast. Within minutes it had engulfed the whole warehouse. The carpets on the ground, the carpets in the aisle, all ablaze. It was scary and fascinating at the same time. I was expecting the sprinklers to come on, but when I looked up, there were none. Nothing was going to stop this fire. The place was enveloped in flame.

Al Butler leapt and grabbed at the camera. His fingers clutched it and he brought it down from the wall angrily.

"There!" he yelled, throwing it across the floor. "Cannae see us now, pal!"

The fire was moving too fast, it seemed to be bouncing from one wall to another, searching for a way out of this enclosed space. And that's when I remembered the shutter door. We had dragged it down, shut ourselves in. We were trapped.

SEVENTEEN

At last I was able to move.

"Gary! The shutters!"

We leapt for the shutter door together, as behind us the fire raged closer.

"Come on, everybody, help!"

I think real panic began to set in then. Even for Al Butler. What if we couldn't get the steel shutter lifted? It wouldn't just be the cameras that would be burnt to a crisp, it would be us, too.

It was harder lifting it this time. We didn't have the same leverage, but determination and fear made us strong. Smoke was beginning to fill the warehouse. The shutter rose slowly at first. And then, once again, it zoomed to the top. We were out of there and into the open in a flash, coughing and spluttering, tears in our eyes from the smoke.

"Come on!" Claude shouted, moving back from the fire step by step. I moved too, back out onto the street. That's when I heard a scream. I looked around. The flames, the smoke had begun to seep into the premises beside the warehouse and the flats above them. And they weren't derelict after all. They weren't empty. People still lived there, worked there. Claude had seen it too.

"Come on!" Baz yelled. I grabbed Gary and we stumbled away from the scene. I was excited, frightened, mesmerised, I can't even explain the emotions that were racing through me as fast as that fire was taking hold. We ran until we were sure we were out of sight, and then we headed for higher ground so we would have a view of the whole block and the fire. We stood for a moment, trying to get our breath back and shaking the smoke from our clothes, watching as a tornado of flames erupted from the warehouse roof. The whole block was now ablaze.

Then, the worst thing, the worst thing ever. People came running from the flats we had thought were empty – from doorways, from the back, from the front. Hurtling down stairs to the street. Through the smoke we could even make out a couple jumping from windows.

"They've got to be out. All of them," I said to Gary.

"Got to be," he said.

In the distance I could hear a siren coming closer. Fire engine? Police? Didn't matter. Time to get out of here.

Al Butler was still with us. He was leaping up and down screaming, "Brilliant! What a night!" Loving the fire, the destruction. This had been his plan all along. He looked mad. The fire reflected in the ice-blue of his eyes gave him the look of something alien, someone not quite human.

Baz was laughing. "They won't need central heating in them flats now."

Was Baz trying to impress Al Butler? I thought he was. Because I surely knew him too well to believe that seeing people flooding from that burning building wasn't worrying him. It was worrying me.

He looked round at me and winked.

"Let's get out of here," I said.

Al Butler didn't move. For him, we weren't even there any more. He still stood, fascinated by the fire. It was the last time I ever saw him.

We were back on the other side of the estate before we stopped running.

The fire lit the night sky. Little fireflies of light floated up into the darkness. Sounds were everywhere; we could hear them in the distance. Sirens and yells, screams, shouts.

"Do you think all those people got out?" Gary's voice was shaking.

"Fire brigade's there, I think they must have. You saw them." Claude squeezed Gary's shoulder, as if to reassure himself as much as Gary that it was true.

"They'll be ok. They'll be ok." I think I was trying to reassure myself too.

Time to go.

Time to get out of here.

EIGHTEEN

My mother was in when I got back. She didn't say a word about me going out, she was just relieved to see me. She had heard rumours about a gang fight somewhere on the estate, and it had worried her. I lied when she asked me if I'd heard about it, told her me and the boys had stayed at the precinct, just chatting, we weren't involved in any fight, this was the first I'd heard about it, I said. Maybe I should have told her the truth then. But I didn't. I didn't want another argument, and she obviously didn't want one either.

"I think I'll just go to bed, Mum."

I don't know how she didn't smell the smoke. I was sure it must have soaked though my clothes and into my skin. If she did, she said nothing about it.

I stood under the spray in the shower for ages, trying to get clean, trying to calm down, stop shaking, trying to stop my heart from thumping. I was still scared, yet I'd never felt so excited. I can't put the feeling into words. How can you have two different feelings at the same time? I kept listening for the police bursting through the door, imagining that they had followed me home, that they knew who I was and what I had done. Imagining that the CCTV camera hadn't been destroyed after all.

I went into my room and flopped on the bed. I couldn't sleep, just kept going over and over all that had happened that night. Dodging the Young Bow, leading them right into a trap with the Dragos. That's how it had started, and it had been exciting, it was smart. Had that only been tonight? So much had happened since then, it seemed a long time ago. We'd run through the streets, our excitement building, the car alarms going off, running again... Then meeting up with that Al Butler, and everything seemed to change. As if it wasn't real any more. We had followed him inside that warehouse; I can see it now with that red glow around us. Just a bit of fun to begin with, until Al Butler had spotted the camera. And suddenly it seemed it was all taken out of our hands.

Over and over in my mind I was in the middle of that fire again. I could feel the heat of it. I saw the orange and red and white flames leaping, dancing, racing through the warehouse, almost as if they were living things searching out what they could touch and destroy. I didn't want to move. I wanted to keep looking.

But I felt sick when I made myself remember the people in the flats nearby. Had all of those people managed to get away? Had the fire been put out? If I'd been the cause of someone being hurt I'd never forgive myself. I had never seriously hurt anyone in my life. I took out my phone, wanted to call Baz, decided against it. Because I bet he didn't feel guilty. And if I wouldn't call Baz, then I wouldn't call any of the others.

Later, I heard Vince coming in. "Heard about the fire?" he asked Mum. As soon as he said it, I sat up in bed. "Massive fire, further up on the estate."

"Oh my goodness, anybody hurt?" my mum asked.

It was a moment before he answered her. Cliffhanger moment. I could imagine him, pulling open the fridge door, taking out the milk, having a swig. He always did that as soon as he came in. Mum always giving him into trouble for it. She didn't give him into trouble now.

I wanted to shout, 'Answer her! Was anybody hurt?'

"Quite a few were taken to hospital. Don't know how serious they are. Big fire though. Started in a carpet warehouse, I heard, then everything round about it went up. Still raging."

"How did it start?"

I held my breath as I waited for his answer.

"Who knows? Always something going on. There was

a big gang fight on the estate as well." He paused. "Is Logan in?"

Right away he was suspicious that I was involved.

"He's been in for ages," Mum said. "Thank goodness."

"Been a busy night on this estate, police everywhere," Vince said.

"Oh, Vince, I wish we would hear about that house," her voice became a worried whisper.

I didn't listen after that. I fell back on the bed. They didn't know who started the fire, not yet. I was a tumble of emotions. Why did Baz dare Al Butler to do it? Why hadn't we tried to stop him? Why did we follow him inside? We could have just helped him lift the shutters, and then run on. Why didn't we? If anybody died because of that fire, I'd... I'd... I couldn't even think about what I would do.

NINETEEN

I went to the same school as Lucie. The other boys all attended the big high school on the estate. I once said to Lucie that I wondered why that was, and she had an easy answer. "This is the loser school. You get sent here if nobody else wants you. Everybody here is a loser, just like you and me. A loser or a weirdo."

"I'm not a weirdo." I'd never to admit to that. "Or a loser."

"Well, I am definitely a bit weird. Can't deny it."

We, both of us, had been excluded more than once. I had run with a bad crowd up in Aberdeen, got into all sorts of bother, and that reputation had followed me here. That was why I still had a social worker. Our school was especially for kids like us. 'Troubled teens' I think they called us.

"We're special," I told Lucie. It was what the social workers were always telling us anyway. "So this is a special school."

"A special school for weirdos!" she had insisted with a giggle. Then she stared at me for a moment in that strange way she had. "You're not as weird when you're on your own," she said. "You should try it more often."

It wasn't the other boys she was talking about. Lucie had never met any of them. It was Baz. I wanted to ask her why she disliked him so much, but I knew the answer to that already. She thought he was a bad influence on me.

Lucie and I usually walked to school together, ate together at break and sat on our own on the steps outside the school entrance for lunch. Always on our own. Even in a school for weirdos we were weirder than the rest, it seemed.

It was easy to see why Lucie was shunned by most of the girls both at school and on the estate. She didn't fit in with them at all. She had no favourite pop band. I don't think she even liked music. She wasn't interested in clothes or make-up. The boys ignored her too. Most of them were a bit scared to talk to her, the rest just didn't like her.

In a way, I was her best friend. Sad state of affairs for anybody.

I met her at one of the corner shops the day after the fire. I'd been dying to be out and hear what was happening. I hadn't slept all night.

"Heard about the fire?" she asked.

It would have been impossible not to have heard about it, it was the top item on the local news that morning. It had taken all night and fire crews from all over the city to contain the blaze.

Did I swallow, did my face go red? "I heard. Did everybody get out?"

"There's a few in the hospital."

"Serious?"

She looked at me in that funny way she had. "Goodness, you're really worried about them, aren't you?"

"I have got a nice side, you know."

She shrugged. "If you say so."

"You seem to know everything. Do you know who started it?"

"It was arson," she said. "Deliberate. That's what they're saying."

"They can't be sure of that." Did I sound guilty? "Dry summer night, easy for things to catch on fire."

Lucie shrugged. "Forensic evidence. They'll know." She fumbled in her rucksack and took out a bottle of juice. Unscrewed the lid and took a long swallow. "And there'll be CCTV footage of course."

CCTV! The very thought of it made me shiver. All of us boldly walking in, and even waving. What had we been thinking about?

"The cameras would have been destroyed in the fire... Wouldn't they?"

I saw the beginnings of real suspicion in her face. "You seem to know a lot about this fire."

"I have an alibi, don't you worry."

"Didn't even know you were a suspect, Logan."

I could feel my face go red. "I'm not. I'm just saying... I was with my pals. I didn't even hear about it till I was home. Vince came in and told us."

Lucie laughed. "Oh well, say you were with your pals and they were with you. Not a lie anyway. You can alibi each other."

"We were just hanging about last night, nowhere near any trouble." I shouldn't have said a word about the fire in the first place. "Anyway, cops wouldn't be interested in boys like us."

Lucie sneered. "Don't be too sure," she said.

When I went home that day, I half-expected the place to be filled with black-uniformed cops in riot gear, waiting for me. Instead, the house was empty. No one was home.

I took out my phone. I called Baz. "Have you heard anything?"

"No, mate," he said. "What are you doing?"

"Nothing. Meet you at the shops?"

"In ten," he said.

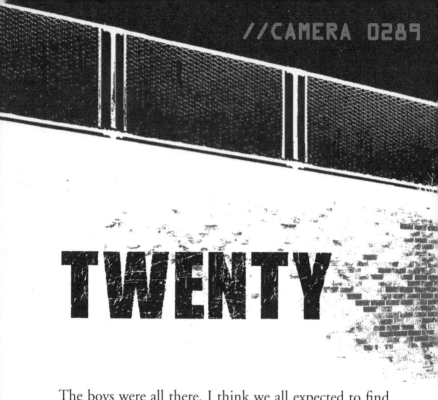

TWENTY

The boys were all there. I think we all expected to find the precinct swarming with cops, but it wasn't. Still, we were nervous.

"I hope those people in the flats are ok." First thing Gary said. "I hadn't even noticed there were flats there."

"I saw them," Mickey said. He had brought Ricky with him, of course. "But I thought they were empty."

"Me too," I said.

"There's a few of them people in hospital."

"I'm not going to feel guilty," Baz broke in. "We didn't start the fire. It was Al Butler. He was aiming to torch that place from the beginning. So nothing was our fault."

He was right, of course. Nothing would have stopped Al Butler. But had Baz forgotten he had dared Al Butler to drop the match – double-dared him? Of course he had, and none of us reminded him.

"The police were at my cousin's, questioning him as to 'his whereabouts last night'." Claude tried to make it sound funny. But nothing was funny that day for us. His cousin was one of the usual suspects. Always the first the police picked up when there was any kind of trouble.

"I would have got a real wallop from my dad if he thought I had anything to do with this." I remembered then Gary saying he had left home a couple of times because of his dad's heavy hand.

The story of the fire had been on the television, it was all people on the estate seemed to be interested in. People walking past us, huddled in groups, all talking about it.

Baz laughed. "Your dad's got some nerve, all the dodgy things he gets involved in."

Gary said nothing. His jaw clenched. If any of us but Baz had said that, I'm sure Gary would have flown at us. Instead, after a moment, he only shrugged. He didn't want a fight. "My dad's never started fires," he said. "My dad's never been arrested. Doesn't expect me to be."

I patted him on the back. "At least you've got a dad who cares about you."

He pulled his shoulder away from me. Gary didn't like me. I didn't think any of them did. Not for the first time I reflected if it hadn't been for Baz they wouldn't have let me near them.

"Do you remember the CCTV camera? Do you think it really was destroyed?" I had almost been afraid to mention that.

Gary nodded. "All I've thought about. We're on that camera. If it wasn't destroyed, they're bound to find out who we are."

Baz broke in confidently. "No, that Al Butler tore it from the wall, remember, and the rest of it melted. Stop worrying about it."

Mickey shook his head. "Anyway, my ma says it's an insurance job. That happens all the time. The owners set deliberate fires then claim the insurance money. End up with more money than the place is worth. The cops won't be looking for us. I'm sure of that."

Ricky let out a yelp and Mickey laughed. "See, Ricky agrees with me."

"Who was that guy last night, Gary, you said you knew him?" It was Mickey who asked.

"Knew *about* him," Gary corrected. "His name's Al Butler. Bad news. I nearly died when I saw him there. Did you see his eyes light up when he watched the fire? He's crazy."

I remembered how blue they looked, bluest eyes I had ever seen.

"I think he's done that before," Claude said.

"I think he has too," Gary said. "He came well

prepared for it anyway." I felt guilty when I thought of my own excitement as I saw the fire taking hold. I wasn't like Al Butler, was I?

"So he would have done that whether we were there or not, eh?" Claude looked around us hopefully, waiting for someone to agree with him.

"We couldn't have stopped him," Baz said. Was he trying to justify daring Al Butler to drop the match?

Did that make it better? That we couldn't have stopped him? We hadn't even stayed to make sure those people did get out safely. We didn't wait to help. No. We were every bit as guilty as Al Butler.

"Do you think the cops'll come after us?" Mickey asked. His dog looked up at him, as if it understood every word.

Baz answered. "Oh come on. We're only boys. Nobody's interested in us. Nobody saw us. I think we should celebrate." He pulled a wad of notes from his pocket. We all gasped.

"Where did you get that?" Claude asked.

Baz grinned. "Remember the Xbox games? Sold them on the way home." I waited for him to tell them I'd been with him when he sold them to a couple of junkies hanging around the underpass. I had wanted him to just throw them away, didn't want anything to do with them. But when did Baz ever listen to me? I was glad that in the end he didn't mention me. "Well come on, look a bit happy about it. They would only have got burned up in the fire. We need cheering up." He was laughing. "The drinks are on me."

So we all ended up in a local burger bar, courtesy of Baz and the Xboxes, burgers all round.

"Love it here!" Baz said. "You get onion rings so big you could wear them as a necklace!"

He was in a great mood, and that was when he was at his best. He took our minds off what had happened. He made us all laugh.

Mickey tied his dog up outside, but it whined so much he left before he'd even finished his burger.

"Take him home and come back," I said. "We're all going to the cinema."

But he shook his head. "Naw, left him last night and the night before. He'll be really upset if I leave him again tonight."

"You'd think he was your girlfriend!" Gary shouted.

"Better than a girlfriend, my Ricky." There was a softness in Mickey you had to like. I watched him walk away, Ricky padding along beside him, looking up at him, as if he was taking in his every word, and I knew Mickey was talking to him the way he always did.

"Him and that dog of his," I laughed.

"Mickey and Ricky!" Baz was laughing. "They could be a double act! Like Laurel and Hardy."

We were all in a much better mood when we went on to the cinema.

We didn't last long in there. Throwing popcorn about,

kicking over cokes, using our phones, annoying everybody. We were all hauled out, and barred from going back.

As soon as we were outside, Gary turned on me. "That was all your fault, why can't you ever just keep quiet?"

"Me?" I said.

"You started all that throwing stuff about. I wanted to see the movie."

Baz stepped in. "You didn't have to join in. Your choice. You could have left... like Mickey."

Gary stepped back. He'd never stand up to Baz. But he still glared at me. "You're nothing but trouble."

He knew the school I went to. They all did. He knew how often I had been excluded. He was waiting for Baz to say something, but he didn't. Neither did I.

Then Gary was off, running down the street. Claude hurried after him, always best friends. "Hey Gary, come back!"

"Don't let Gary bother you," Baz said as we walked home.

I wanted to say, *He only puts up with me 'cause you're here*. But how pathetic would that sound? I wanted too to ask why on earth Baz liked me. No one else seemed to. But how pathetic would that sound as well?

It was as if he read my mind. "You and me are alike, Logan. I know we're completely different, but somewhere in here," he tapped his head, "we're exactly the same. Don't worry, I won't desert you. You'll always have me."

Then Baz left, taking the path behind the shops to his place. One last wave, and he was gone.

A second later, he popped his head round the corner again. "Well, not tonight you won't have me of course, I've gotta go home... but I'll be back tomorrow. And then I won't desert you!" I could hear his roaring laugh as he disappeared again.

He had made me feel good. I wouldn't let Gary spoil my mood. As I lay in bed that night and looked back on everything, now that we were out of danger, I realised it had been a great weekend. Exciting, dangerous, and we hadn't been caught. We wouldn't be caught. And I tried to push the surveillance camera and the people still in hospital to the back of my mind.

TWENTY-ONE

My mother works in a call centre. Did I already tell you that? I might have. I told them I wouldn't be good at writing all this down. Anyway, she's the one who supports the whole family. I should respect her for that. But I never did. I thought she was a mug. Her boyfriend, husband, whatever, Vince, he's an ex-soldier, dishonourable discharge if you ask me, though of course he would never admit to it. He was invalided out, according to him. There's nothing wrong with him that I can see. He's just lazy. And as for that son of his, thank goodness I don't have to share a room with him any more. He's off to train to be a soldier too. Just like his dad.

Don't know what the army's coming to with soldiers like that. No wonder we lost an empire.

Both Mum and Vince were out the night I heard the news on TV. It was a couple of days after the fire. Mum was on a late shift; don't know where Vince was. I'd been trying to avoid watching the television, always worried that they might show my face from the CCTV footage, rescued somehow from the warehouse. All I did know was some of the residents from the flats were still in hospital. I was just sitting down to my tea when the news came on, and the fire was the first item. It was on before I could switch over to another channel.

"Whoever did this will be caught," a policeman said. "The response from the public has been excellent. We do have suspects. We are pursuing all leads."

Suspects? Was he talking about us?

There was an Asian man interviewed, his fire-damaged shop behind him. It had been on the other side of the block, but not far enough away to escape the flames. "This shop was my livelihood," he was saying. "Now, I will have to begin again."

"You must be very angry about that," the reporter asked him.

But the man shook his head. "I believe in karma. What goes around, comes around. They will repay in another way for what they have done." He said it very quietly, it was softly spoken, yet his words sent a chill through me.

Karma.

I knew it would freak me out, but I couldn't stop watching. I had to hear everything they'd say.

And then they went back to the night of the fire. I had to look. My eyes were drawn to the screen.

The warehouse was ablaze, and everything around it too: mountains of flames billowing into the sky. Fire engines were there, tackling the blaze, firemen balanced on the tops of ladders, their hoses shooting water over the flames. Then the same reporter came on again with the backdrop of the ruined wreck of the building behind him, still smouldering.

Did I feel guilty?

Yes, guilty about the people in the flats. Guilty about the Asian man who had lost his livelihood. But not about the warehouse itself. Hadn't Mickey said the owners would claim insurance and end up with more money than it was worth?

Then the screen focused on one man. The reporter introduced him as the owner of the warehouse where the fire had started. An old man, he looked tired, as if he'd been up all night. But there was something more than tiredness in his voice. There was anger.

He stared right into the camera, and when he spoke, his voice didn't sound old, it was cold as ice. "I'm telling you out there, the people who did this, if you're watching," he paused, "you *will* be caught."

"Have you any idea who might be responsible for this?" the reporter asked.

The old man didn't even glance at him. He kept his eyes fixed on the camera. I felt he was looking straight at me. It was me he was talking to.

"I just want them to know. If they're watching. You won't escape justice. *Don't for a moment think you're safe.*"

TWENTY-TWO

I couldn't get those words out of mind. *Don't for a moment think you're safe.*

In my dreams that night they were coming closer, cloaked and masked, men in black heading my way, so that I woke with a start, sure they were in my room, standing in the corner, watching me.

Everywhere I went over the next few days, I imagined them waiting for me. They knew where I lived. They were following me. I was always looking over my shoulder.

I almost ran into Lucie one day at the shops, bowling her over because I wasn't looking where I was going. "Are you expecting someone?" Lucie's gaze followed mine.

She had noticed a change in me. She had told me as much at school. I had avoided going home with her, afraid that if these imaginary men saw me with her, she might be in danger too. I looked guilty at that moment, I know I did. But I only told her I was having more arguments with my mum and Vince, and she seemed to accept that. I didn't want to talk to her in case I blurted out the truth.

I almost said I was waiting for Baz, then changed my mind. I never even mentioned Baz's name to her. She had no time for him.

It was later that day before I met up with Baz and the boys. I hadn't seen any of them since the burger bar, and it turned out I wasn't the only one who had watched that item on the news. Claude and Gary had too. "What do you think he meant?" Claude asked. "'Don't for a moment think you're safe.' What's that all about?"

Gary was even more bothered about it than I was. "I wish we'd never went into that place."

In front of the boys, I didn't want to look as scared as I felt.

It was Baz who spoke: "He was an old man. Talking rubbish."

"He said it as if he meant it," Gary said. "And he'll have sons."

"Don't get your knickers in a twist," Baz said. "The old geezer had to say something. Had to sound hard."

He laughed, and so did I. "You don't think you could handle an old geezer like him if he came after you?"

It was a dare he threw at the rest of us. He began stumbling about like an old man, waving an imaginary cane in the air. His voice was scratched and sickly. "You boys... In my young day, you would have been caned, got the birch! The birch, I tell you. Or capital punishment – aye, that's what you need. You wouldn't do it again after that, eh?"

Why did Baz always make me feel better? He wasn't scared. So why should I be? He was right. I had made too much of that old man's comments. So had Gary and Claude. The old man had to say something, didn't he?

"Just remember," Baz said. "That camera was destroyed in the fire, but even if anything was left, CCTV's always fuzzy. Even if they've got it, they won't make us out, and anyway we've not got a criminal record. How are the police gonny find us?"

Lucie was at the park as I walked home. Looking lost, swinging her legs. It was almost dark.

"Shouldn't you be home?" I asked her.

She checked her watch. "Shouldn't you?"

I never quite got an answer from Lucie.

"Police were at my place," she said.

"At your house?"

She shook her head; a clasp fell from her hair. "Not

mine, but along our balcony. You could hardly miss them, clomping about with their big feet. They're checking up on everybody."

"Not me, or you," I said quickly.

"Bide your time," Lucie said. "You don't think you weren't spotted? Caught on camera?"

And I remembered again the old man on the television. Shook the thought of him away.

"Spotted doing what?" I asked her. "I haven't done anything."

She shrugged. "If you say so."

"I do say so."

"My mum says I shouldn't talk to you. She says you're trouble."

"Me?" I said. "I've never even met your mum. What makes her think I'm trouble? What have you been telling her?"

She didn't answer that. Instead she said. "You're not bad when you're like this."

"Like what?" I asked.

She waved her hands around as if she was trying to snatch the right words out of the air. "On your own," she said at last.

"You think maybe some people are a bad influence on me?" She was meaning Baz, of course. I knew she was.

"Maybe you're the one," Lucie said, "who's a bad influence on other people."

I kicked at stones as I walked away from her. Sometimes Lucie said things that made me think. This was one of those times. Lucie bothered me. More than I would ever admit to anyone.

TWENTY-THREE

Over those days after the fire, the estate teemed with police. They seemed to be everywhere. Some of the older boys were taken in for questioning. I kept wondering if Al Butler was too. Maybe they had him in custody already. Then I would start to worry about what he might tell them about us. But no, if he told them about us, he would have to admit he was at the warehouse.

News about the fire was constantly on television. Questions being asked. Questions answered. Each time I caught sight of a news bulletin I held my breath, waiting to see that old man's face again, hear his words: 'Don't for a moment think you're safe.'

But he never appeared. I began to feel I had only imagined it.

I watched a Crimewatch programme one night and CCTV images appeared, hardened criminals the whole country was looking for, menacing hooded figures with scowling faces, every one of them with a number printed underneath. Would my number come up soon?

But there were never any images of us. We were safe.

The days passed, the residents of the burnt-out flats were all discharged from hospital, and no one came after us. Not the police, nor that old man. In my mind he grew older. His face became more wrinkled, like a withered apple, his skin grey, his jaws slack. He was a pantomime old man, wagging his bent bony fingers at me. We had nothing to fear. We were young. We were invincible.

"Who's up for a day out tomorrow? Hey, it's Saturday. We got no school to go to." It was Baz who suggested it. "And we've got something to celebrate, the cops are looking everywhere... except at us. We weren't caught. What did I tell you?"

Hadn't I been thinking the same thing? "Yeah, come on, one day out for the boys. All those people from the fire, they're all out of hospital, did you hear?"

Mickey nodded. "And they're saying it was definitely an insurance job now. They've got the owner in for questioning, I heard."

That was news – great news – to me. "Are they really?"

"They found traces of that lighter fluid, even the bottle it was in, so they know it was deliberate, so now it's the owners they're after."

The owners? That old man? I felt a touch of guilt about an innocent man being blamed for something he didn't do. But I shook the thought of him away. Now there was no chance of him coming after us, was there? He would have enough to contend with convincing the police he had nothing to do with the fire, so he'd have less time to worry about us, wouldn't he?

"Ok, day out," Claude said. "Where will we go?"

"Into the city," Gary said at once. "Where else would you go for a day out?"

"Into Glasgow?" Mickey looked baffled, as if we had just suggested a trip to the moon.

"You're talking as if you've never been there," Claude laughed.

"I never have."

"Oh come on! You, Mickey?" Gary sounded astonished. "I mean, I can understand Logan here never having been in, but you! You're a native Glaswegian."

"Well, I've never been into the city. Ok?"

"It'll be good," I said, glad that for once I wasn't the only one who was an outsider. "I'm dying to see it." I felt excited at the thought.

"Hey! We're going to have an adventure!" Baz shouted.

"Are you paying?" Gary asked.

It was Baz who answered. "Me? Pay? Hey, you're my

116

mate, entitled to my liver and one of my kidneys, but keep your hands off my money."

It made us all laugh. Typical Baz.

Mickey was a bit reluctant at first, but after a while he was up for it too. He wanted to take his perishing dog with him, but we persuaded him maybe it wasn't a good idea. So it was decided: we would meet at the precinct next morning and head to the station and take the train into the city.

TWENTY-FOUR

Baz was going to meet me at my flats first, but I waited and waited, and finally gave up on him. I didn't want to miss the boys at the precinct. Didn't want them going without me. So maybe I didn't wait as long as I should have. I tried to call Baz, but his phone went straight onto voicemail. And, do you know what? I was relieved. It took me a while to realise that was how I felt. But I knew I wasn't disappointed that he wasn't there. And as I headed to meet the other boys at the precinct, I kept hoping that Baz wouldn't be with them either.

None of the others even mentioned him. I think they felt the same. I was in a great mood, didn't want anything to spoil it. And I felt guilty even thinking this, but Baz might have spoiled things.

We had to pass close to the burnt-out warehouse to get to the station. No way to avoid it. For the first time I could see what remained of the flats on the other side of that block, and a couple of shops too. All empty and blackened. There was one shop still open, right on the corner. I was sure this was the one owned by the Asian man I'd seen on TV. It had a sign on the door.

So many people were there sweeping up, cleaning the place up, helping to move things out or carry things in, decent people, standing by a neighbour in trouble.

The four of us went quiet as we walked past. We kept our heads down guiltily and we didn't say a word.

The station was busy with people. Women heading into town for shopping, families going for a day out. I liked trains. We'd come down from Aberdeen on the train, and that was an amazing journey. I was glad none of the boys had suggested taking the underground into the city. I would feel trapped in there. They all laughed at me when I told them.

"That's a great way to travel through Glasgow," Gary said. "Fast and cheap. Nothing to beat it."

"I used to read stories about people trapped in the underground. Down in London. They would go down there during the Blitz. Sings songs to cheer themselves up while the Luftwaffe bombed their houses up top. I don't think singing would have cheered me up."

"Must have been scary, but," Mickey said. "If a bomb hit when you were down there you'd never get out. Trapped underground? My idea of hell."

"Mine too, Mickey," I agreed. "If I was gonny die it would be out in the open air. Not under the ground." I was totally creeped out by the very thought of it.

We were still chatting as the train pulled into Queen Street Station. It had taken us right into the centre of the city. How exciting was that! We came out into a great square, surrounded by impressive, grand-looking grey buildings. "This is George Square," Gary told me. "This is where they filmed World War Z! Thousands of zombies in Glasgow. Have you seen it?"

Of course we all had. That set us off running round the square snarling like the undead. Some people smiled at us, others moved away. Maybe they thought we really were zombies.

I'd lived here for a couple of months and never once come into the city. I wanted to take one of the tour buses, but I found out that Gary knew so much about Glasgow, and not just about zombies, so who needed a bus?

"Walking's the best way to see anywhere in Glasgow," he assured us.

We couldn't have picked a better day. The sun was shining, everyone seemed to be smiling. There was a wonderful feeling in the air. We walked down West George Street, and the first thing I spotted was a statue of some guy on a horse with a traffic cone on his head.

"That's Wellington," Gary said. "They're always trying to stop people doing that: the traffic cone gets taken off, but next day... there's another traffic cone stuck on his head again."

"I hope they never stop them," I said, because I thought it was so brilliant. "That's just Glasgow, isn't it?"

"Fantastic!" Gary said, and he began to run. "Come on, let's go to the river."

TWENTY-FIVE

So we wound our way through the pedestrian precincts and the streets, passing musicians and beggars and acrobats. We stopped a few times to watch their shows, then ran like crazy when they came round with the hat for money. Finally we came to the river. The Clyde sparkled in the sun, and the bridges spanning the river glittered like silver.

"There's the Squinty Bridge."

Gary didn't even have to point it out, it was so plain to see. Its reflection on the river made a shape like a perfect egg.

"It's actually called something else." Gary searched his memory for the name. Snapped his fingers when it came to him: "The Clyde Arc, that's its name. But here in Glasgow we just call it the Squinty Bridge."

"Typical Glasgow." I was beginning to like this Glasgow, with its sense of humour and the way they never seemed to take anything seriously. I was beginning to admire Gary even more too. This was a different side to him, a side I'd never seen before. "You really know your stuff, Gary."

We walked on towards the bridge. "My dad, he's really proud of this city. He's always taking us places, telling us stories about it."

I felt a sudden wave of sadness. I had once had a dad like that too. I brushed the feeling away. I didn't want anything to spoil this day. Instead I said, "Good, you're a perfect tour guide, then."

So we took the walkway along the Clyde and then headed over the bridge. Gary was a blinking encyclopedia of information. He could tell us all the horrible ways men died in the shipyards that had once been here, and the ships that had been built and launched on the river. "Glasgow is the fourth-largest city in Britain, and it used to be called 'the Second City of the Empire'."

"When we had an Empire!" I laughed. "How do you know all this stuff?"

"My dad can trace our family right back to the time of William Wallace."

I laughed. "Aye, and they were selling dodgy goods then as well, I bet."

Gary looked at me, his face suddenly serious. I patted him on the back. "Shouldn't have said that, Gary. No offence." I didn't want anything to spoil our day, and, after a moment, he laughed too.

"William Wallace?" Claude had been thinking about this. "I've heard of him. Was he the one with the spider?" And then he had us all laughing like idiots.

"What about you, Logan?" Gary asked me.

"Me? I come from a long line of Scottish peasants, some Irish too, I think. Nothing interesting."

"I've definitely got Welsh blood in me," Mickey said proudly. "That's how I'm such a good singer." Then he began to treat us to a rendition of Bohemian Rhapsody. *"I'm just a poor boy from a poor family..."* The rest of us put our hands over our ears and ran. Mickey ran after us, still singing at the top of his voice. Finally he shut up and went into a coughing fit. "Welsh blood, and I can't sing for toffee," he said proudly.

Gary started to laugh loudly. Had us all joining in. "That's a violation of the Trades Description Act." He turned to me. "What about you, Logan? Any talents we should know about?"

"Well, I play football like a one-legged horse. Does that count?"

"My dad says that's the kind of horse he always backs in the Grand National," said Gary.

"I never knew my daddy." Claude sounded kind of wistful. "Never really needed him. My ma is all I ever needed, me and my sister, Taylor. My ma probably frightened my dad away. She scares most people." Then he laughed. "My ma is one really scary lady." He said it with pride.

"Where's your dad?" Gary asked me.

"Took one look at me and dropped dead," I told him. Actually, he had died when I was ten, and he had been just a boy himself when I was born. But I remembered him, still missed him every day.

"Your mum's married again though, isn't she?"

I didn't want to think about that. There was never a man in my mother's life after my dad. She'd been as broken-hearted as me when he had died. It had just been her and me until this Vince had come along.

"I suppose..." I still hated to acknowledge a marriage. I spat on the pavement. "I mean, getting married again... at her age."

"I never want to get married," Mickey said. "As long as I've got Ricky, I'm happy." And that set us all off laughing again.

I learned more about Gary and Claude and Mickey that day than I had learned since I'd first met them. And they learned about me. We talked the whole day as we walked round the city. Talked and laughed. There was no tension between us at all. Why was that? Only one answer came to mind. Baz. When Baz was there we never talked like this.

We ended up at the cinema, and Gary warned me

before we went in. "No funny stuff. Don't want chucked out again, eh?"

I had to hold in the beginning of anger about that. Until I realised he was right. That night before at the cinema I had behaved that way to impress Baz. Baz wasn't here, so I didn't have to impress anybody.

On the way home on the train we were treated to a spectacular gold and red sunset. The end of a perfect day.

We parted at the precinct, to go our separate ways.

"Been a great day," Gary said.

"Yeah," I agreed. "Been terrific."

Gary patted me on the back as we parted. "Should always be like this, pal."

It should always be like this. Why wasn't it? Because of Baz. We were all afraid of him, afraid to go against him. If he wasn't here permanently, what would happen?

I tried to stop myself thinking like that. It seemed like a betrayal. But it was hard not to. That day was so good. We had laughed together, and talked together. And with no Baz there... it was better.

TWENTY-SIX

I could hear Vince and my mum in the living room. They were laughing, getting ready to go out. It was some anniversary or other. I sat in my room waiting for them to leave. Mum popped her head round the door. "You sure you don't want to come?" She'd been asking me all day.

I didn't want her to press me to go, so I smiled. "No, Mum. Go, have a nice time."

Things had been better between us over the past couple of days. Mum and I had talked and laughed, and I knew that pleased her. I hadn't contacted Baz, nor he me. Was that why it had been better? After the day out I had had with the boys, I didn't want to see him.

Mum didn't insist I go with her. She only hesitated a moment longer before she said, "Plenty in the fridge for you to eat. We won't be late."

I waited till I heard the door closing behind them before I moved into the living room. I grabbed some milk and made myself a sandwich, then I flopped onto the couch. I relished the luxury of it, having the house to myself. And the remote control. Being able to choose what I wanted to watch. I switched on the TV and began flicking through the channels. I was looking for something with a bit of action in it. Eventually I found an old vampire movie and settled in to watch.

I jumped when my phone buzzed. Gary's name came up on the screen. Gary? Calling me? Gary seldom called me. I snapped it open. "What is it?"

Gary's voice was only slightly louder than a whisper. "Have you got the evening paper there?"

I looked around. Vince always brought in the Glasgow evening paper. It was lying folded on the chair. "Yes, it's here," I said, lifting it.

I could hear Gary breathing nervously. "Page five. Turn to page five. Read it and phone me back."

And then he was gone.

I had no doubt the item was about the fire. Why else would he call me? Surely we already knew all there was to know? Could there be any more surprises? I flicked over the pages.

The story actually took up two pages: four and five.

On one side there were two photos: one of the blazing flames of the buildings, and another of a grim man who looked like a horse. He was stepping inside the police station, and waving away microphones.

'MAD MIKE' ANGRY AT FIRE

The warehouse fire at a Glasgow estate has now been confirmed as arson. We understand that a man was taken in for questioning yesterday, but has been released today without charge. The man's name is Michael Machan, sometimes referred to as 'Mad Mike'. He is the son of the warehouse owner, and was arrested fifteen years ago on charges relating to organised crime, but the charges were eventually dropped when two key witnesses withdrew their statements.

Mr Machan vehemently denies any involvement in this fire. In a statement read by a family spokesperson, Mr Machan declared his anger at the destruction of their property and at the police investigation. He said the family were taking the incident as, 'an attack on their authority'.

A councillor from the estate spoke of his concern over the potential for this incident to escalate further:

'The Machans own half the properties here. They have a great deal of… control. If this is arson, and it *wasn't* the Machans who were responsible, if someone else deliberately set fire to their property, do you think they're going to just let this go? I'm afraid I don't think so. Not the Machans. They don't forgive or forget. I think there are people out there who should be hoping that the police get to them before the Machans do.'

I called Gary back as soon as I'd read it. "I've never heard of this Mad Mike. Who is he?"

"He's the head of one of the worst gangster families in Glasgow. He started off small time – my dad says he remembers when Mad Mike just ran protection rackets, you know, he made shopkeepers pay him to stop anybody robbing them. Then he would buy the properties of the people he was supposed to be protecting. Didn't give them much choice: it was 'Sell, or else…'"

"On this estate?"

"To begin with, but then he moved on to big-time drug dealing. But he's never been convicted of anything. There's always somebody willing to give him an alibi..."

"Or else…?" I said.

Gary quickly agreed. "Aye, Logan, or else. He's a real bad guy. You don't even want to know the things he's done to people who have crossed him. He's terrifying, Logan. My dad read that article and he said Mad Mike is not going to like the fact he was taken in for questioning. My dad says..." He paused again; I could hear him swallow nervously. "My dad says he's not going to give up until he gets who did it... And that's us, Logan."

TWENTY-SEVEN

I lay in bed that night, and couldn't stop thinking about what Gary had told me. An old man threatening to come after you was one thing, but Glasgow gangsters? And maybe, just maybe, that was what the old man had meant: 'Don't for a moment think you're safe'. We weren't safe because his sons would come and get us, and his sons were the Machans.

I'd read about the Krays, those notorious London gangsters, seen programmes about them on television too – the terrible things they'd done to people who stood against them, the terrible tortures they'd inflicted on people. It flashed through my mind as if I was watching a film. But it couldn't happen in real life. Not to me.

Still, I couldn't get it out of my mind that it just might. I almost phoned Baz, but that would have been stupid. I knew what he would say. Could hear him: 'Hey, Gary told you that? You and Gary, you worry too much, brother. Gangsters? Hey, come on. Get real.'

Scared of nothing was Baz, at least on the outside. Was he ever as scared as me on the inside?

By the time Mum came back from her big night out I was sweating with fear. She came into my room. I could see she was a little tipsy. Her face flushed, her eyes sparkling. I sometimes forget how pretty my mum is. She has blonde hair, keeps it short, and has what has to be called a rosebud mouth. That mouth was smiling now. "You not sleeping yet?" She sat on my bed, ran her fingers through my hair, felt the sweat on my brow.

"You feel a little hot. Are you all right?"

No, I wanted to tell her. *I feel sick, sick and scared.* But I said nothing.

"I love you so much, Logan. You know that, don't you?"

At that moment I did know. Had no doubts. She did love me. She'd never stopped loving me. She bent and kissed my brow. "Put your TV off. Get to sleep. It's late."

I looked at her. She was my mother, I should be able to talk to her, tell her my worries. If she really loved me she would do what I wanted, wouldn't she? "I want to go back to Aberdeen," I said. *Away from here*, I was thinking, *far away*. Away from any fear of gangsters coming after me. They wouldn't be able to find me there.

Her tipsy smile disappeared. Her mouth grew tight. Exasperation took its place. "What brought this on?" She shook her head. "I thought you were beginning to like it here. How can you change so quickly?" She let out a long sigh. "We can't go back, Logan. That's not possible, son. You know that."

Because of Vince, that was why it wasn't possible. "You care about your boyfriend more than you care about me."

"I don't. You know that's not true. And he's my husband, Logan. Why can't you accept that?" She sighed. "You know why we moved here, Logan. Remember what happened in Aberdeen? All I've ever done has been for you. We're moving away from here soon anyway. We're going to have a new house. In a really nice area. Vince is just waiting for word about it. You'll see: things will get better then. I wish you would talk to Vince. You know, he does want to be a father to you."

That just made me mad. "I don't want a father. I had one."

"Oh Logan, son. I know how hard it is for you to get over that. But he's gone. He won't come back. We both have to face that." She tried to stroke my brow again. I pushed her hand away. There was no point talking to her. She never listened, not to me. I turned my face to the wall, but she still sat there. Didn't move until Vince called out to her.

"Marie, honey?" he was a little tipsy too.

And of course, when he called, she went.

"Lights out," she said, and she closed the door. Giving up on me, way too early.

TWENTY-EIGHT

Next evening, once I met up with Baz and talked to him, I felt better. I knew I would. At times like this, when I was scared, he was the one I needed. He was always strong and confident. He was on the walkway, waiting for me when I left the house. I blurted out everything that had been in that newspaper.

"Nobody saw us, Logan," he said. "Mate, you worry too much about everything."

He was right about that, it was true. I did.

He slapped me on the back. "That article, it's like cop propaganda. It sells papers. They have to say something because they can't catch anybody. So they put the fear of death into you so you'll give yourself up." He mocked a posh voice. "'Just hope the cops get you before the gangsters do.' Ha! Never heard such tosh."

When he said it like that, of course he was right. By the time we met up with the other boys I was filled with as much bravado as Baz.

Gary looked even more worried than I had been. He began to rattle off to the boys everything he'd told me about the Machans.

Baz interrupted him. "You're overreacting. What do you think this is, a Quentin Tarantino movie?"

Gary got angry. "Even my dad says anybody who touched their properties better watch out. Nobody messes with the Machans. That Mad Mike doesn't like any involvement with the police. For that alone he'll find whoever torched that warehouse and come after them, that's what my dad said. He doesn't know I'm one of them. I'm too scared to tell him. But he said whoever it is should go to the cops. They'd be safer then."

Baz grabbed Gary by the collar. "Well, if the cops come looking for us, we'll know who to blame."

Gary shook himself free. "I'm not a grass. Never would be."

"Better not be." Baz's voice was cold. He stepped back.

"We don't want to be fighting amongst ourselves," said Mickey. "Come on, no point worrying about something that might never happen." His dog started barking, as if it sensed the aggression building up between us.

I was worried that we all might fall apart. And I felt guilty for even thinking it, but I thought Baz would be the cause of it if we did. He didn't seem to understand how scared we felt.

TWENTY-NINE

"You went without me," Baz said. We were walking home having left the other boys to go their separate ways. It hadn't been a good night. We'd all been on the verge of arguing.

I'd almost forgotten our day out to Glasgow. "Where were you?" I asked him.

He didn't answer, just said, "You might have phoned me."

"I did. You didn't answer."

"I never heard the phone."

"I did phone, honest," I said, as if I needed to prove it.

Why couldn't I just say what he would say? Like, *Why didn't* you *phone me?*

He grunted. "Where did you go?" he asked after a while.

"Just into the city. You know, cinema then a burger."

He only nodded. He was annoyed that we'd gone without him, though he wouldn't tell me where *he'd* been.

"I got there," he said. "And you lot had flown the coop."

I so wished he'd stop talking about it. "Waited for ages for you." My voice sounded shaky. I could see he wasn't going to let it go.

"You could have kept phoning me," he said again.

Phones work both ways. That's what I wanted to say. Why couldn't I? And know what I said instead? "Sorry."

He turned his dark eyes on me, and with that look I knew why I'd rather have Baz as my friend than my enemy. I was scared of Baz. Scared to go against him. Scared to annoy him.

Then, all of a sudden, his face broke into a wide grin. "I probably had a better time than you anyway."

I nodded and smiled back as if I agreed with him. Glad the tension was over. And yet, he still didn't tell me where he'd been. And I didn't ask.

That was the last night I had a good night's sleep.

Gary phoned me next day; I'd just come in from school. He was breathless, as if he'd been running. Or as if he was scared. "Meet me at the precinct, Logan? I'm there now."

I knew as soon as I saw him something had happened. He was jumping from one foot to the other and his face was ashen.

"What's wrong?"

"Have you seen this? Have you seen the news?" He whipped out his phone. I saw that his hand was shaking. "Saw it on the way back from school."

He tapped into

BREAKING UK NEWS.

Man's Body Found

I read on.

> A man's body has been found on waste ground in the South Side of Glasgow in what looks like a gangland execution. He was buried in a shallow grave and had one bullet wound to the head.

I shrugged. "So?"

"Wait," he said. He was breathing so fast I thought he was about to hyperventilate.

He scrolled down and a moment later a photograph

appeared. It looked like someone out of Crimewatch: a grainy, unsmiling face staring out of that small screen.

I almost said 'Who is this?' But I didn't, because there was something familiar in that face. I'd seen it before. Where?

"Recognise him?" Gary asked.

I didn't answer. In that second I knew him. The photo was in black and white, but I could still imagine those so-blue eyes staring out at me.

Gary answered his own question. "Al Butler. The man at the fire, the guy who torched the warehouse. Remember him now?"

He'd been smiling that night. Now he'd never smile again.

Gary snapped his phone off. "Don't try and tell me now that nobody saw us that night. That we weren't spotted. 'Gangland execution' – that's what it says. The gangsters got him."

I'd never seen Gary like this, shaking, scared. "He was with us, and they got him."

"You don't know that," I said.

"Did you see what that report said? It was a gangster-style execution. That was how they described it. Gangland execution. Had to be the Machans. And they're coming after us next."

I tried to calm him down. "He was older than us. A lot older. And look at that photo. It was a mug shot. You said yourself, Al Butler was a well-known criminal.

He probably had lots of enemies. We've never been in trouble. No mug shots of us. We're invisible. How could they know we were there?"

"I'll tell you how they know. CCTV."

"The camera was destroyed in the fire, and the police haven't even mentioned CCTV."

"And I'll tell you why. My dad told me last night. Something we didn't even think about. I didn't even know." He slapped his head as if he was some dumbnut. "It didn't matter if the camera was destroyed. It was all going onto a tape, a tape with our faces all over it. The tape isn't in the camera, it's not even usually in the same building. And it'll be the Machans who have got that tape, not the police. That's why the police have never mentioned surveillance cameras. The cameras weren't set up by the police or by some security firm, they were set up by the Machans. And we're all over the tape along with Al Butler."

My stomach turned, my mouth went dry. The cameras didn't matter, not if we were on the tape. "But we didn't do anything."

Gary was shaking with fear. I'd never seen him like this. "We were there with Al Butler. He called us 'his boys', remember? We should go to the cops. They'll give us protection."

Baz was all at once at my shoulder as if he'd come from nowhere. His hand shot out and grabbed Gary by the neck. It happened so fast it took him completely by surprise. Me too. "You better not even think that. You try that and I'll be the one to get you. And I'll be worse than any of them gangsters."

Gary pulled himself free. I stepped in between him and Baz. Didn't want Baz to grab him again.

"It will be ok, Gary. We'll watch out for each other. I'm scared too, but we can't lose it now."

Gary began to back away, but he was shouting at Baz. "What is it with you! You're crazy!" and then he was gone. His feet pounding on the pavement.

"You shouldn't have said that to him, Baz," I said. "He's our mate. He'd never betray us. And he was your mate before mine. You should know that."

"He goes to the cops he'll get us all in trouble." Baz would never admit he'd done anything wrong.

"Do you think he will? Go to the cops, I mean."

He seemed to think about it, then he dismissed it. "Naw. Not Gary. All talk, him."

I believed him because I wanted to believe him. But I didn't sleep that night. Not a wink.

THIRTY

I wished I could tell someone in my family what I was afraid of – wished I had a family to tell. But my mum was too wrapped up in Vince and her job. And if I told her about this, I'd have to tell her I was there when the fire was started. Too complicated. And I couldn't go to the police – I'd gotten into too much trouble in Aberdeen. I was on my final warning. Who had told me that? I couldn't remember.

If I had a dad... It was at times like this I missed having a dad most. If he was here, I could tell him everything, and in my mind I could see him again, as clear as if he was standing in front of me. I remembered him – smiling, handsome, a bit wild, and if he was still alive all this wouldn't have happened. I still had faint memories of him taking me places. Fishing and camping and football. Taking me on days out to the shore in Aberdeen. We used to fly kites – I could almost see them again, lifted up by the wind as we ran along the white sands of the beach. He was always there for me. If he hadn't died, I wouldn't have moved to Glasgow. I'd still be in Aberdeen. We'd still be a family. Everything would be different.

I couldn't confide my fear to Baz. He was the last one I could talk to, and I couldn't talk to any of the other boys behind his back. That would be a betrayal of Baz, and I couldn't do that.

But Lucie was different, in more ways than one. As I waited for her next day, I decided she was the one person I could tell. I watched for her coming along the walkway of her flats, and waved at her. She waved back and came bouncing down the stairs and headed for me. As soon as she saw my face, she knew something was wrong. I obviously can't hide fear very well. "Got a problem?"

"Is it that obvious?"

"Sad thing to say, but I can read you like a book. Not a very interesting one, mind you."

That made me smile. "I'm about the only friend you've got, Lucie."

"Look who's talking!"

"I've got friends." Did I snap it out? I think I did.

She stopped walking. "Are you sure they're friends?"

"Yeah, they're friends. Good friends."

"So, Mr Popular-with-all-the-friends, what's bothering you then?"

I took a deep breath. "Did you see that photo on television? That man who was murdered." The story had made the television news the night before.

She curled her lip. "Been a lot of murders."

"You know the one I mean. His body was found in a shallow grave, bullet through the head."

"So what's that got to do with you?"

"I saw him that night, at that big fire." It was the first time I had talked about it to anyone besides the boys.

"Ah," she said, "it all becomes clear. Were you with him? Did you know him?"

"Yes to the first. No to the second. But he was there, Lucie, and so were we."

I pictured him again, as he was that night, surrounded by fire, his face wild, howling like an animal.

Did he howl again before the gangsters shot him?

Lucie put a finger to her brow. She fired an imaginary shot, then blew on her finger. "They say it was gangsters?"

"Gangland execution."

"So, what have you got to do with gangsters?"

I began to tell her almost everything: about the fire, and about the story I'd read in the paper. "I don't know how it happened, Lucie. We were all caught up in it before we knew what was happening. But we didn't do anything, not really. We were just there."

It was Baz who dared him to drop the match. But I could never betray Baz by telling her that.

"I understand, Logan."

"I'm scared, Lucie. If it was these gangsters got him..."

I didn't have to finish. Lucie finished for me. "If it's the Machans who have the tapes, and they saw him, they must have seen you too. Is that what you're thinking?"

I nodded. "I know you're going to say: I'm overreacting." But Lucie never said anything you expected.

"I'd be thinking the same thing, if I were you. I'd be scared stiff. But maybe he was the only one caught on the camera?" I knew that wasn't true. I remembered us all running in, and even waving boldly at the cameras. How stupid. "It would be easy for them to find this Al Butler." Lucie was trying to make me feel better. "He was well known for all the wrong reasons. But you lot? How could they trace you? How could they find you? None of you have a record... do you?"

Did I? Surely the trouble I had got into in Aberdeen didn't count. I was a juvenile. Even gangsters couldn't access anything from juvenile records, could they?

Lucie touched my arm, still doing her best to reassure me. "You're just small fry," she said. "*Boys*, I have to remind you. You are just boys."

"That's what I'm trying to tell myself."

"And I suppose there's no point saying you should go to the police?"

My expression told her what I thought about that suggestion. "No way."

"Maybe nothing else will happen, Logan. No point worrying about it now. But, I think you should stay away from those friends of yours. For a while anyway."

"One in particular? Is that what you're saying?"

She couldn't look me in the eye. Avoided the question. "I just think you're easily led, Logan. Sorry if that offends you, but you are. And look what's happened."

All day I thought about what she said. And as I walked home I was trying to tell myself that she was right. Baz, I was really beginning to realise, was a bad influence. He had dared us to follow Al Butler into that building, he had dared him to drop the match. I did things to please him, to impress him. We all did. But you can't go blaming other people for what you do wrong. You have to take responsibility for your own actions. My social worker in Aberdeen had told me that. I should have stood up and said I wasn't following Al Butler into that warehouse that night. I should have walked away. But I didn't. Lucie was right. I was easily led. That was how I had got into so much trouble in Aberdeen. I didn't have the kind of courage to stand up to boys like Baz. But I wasn't the only one. The other boys didn't stand up to Baz either.

THIRTY-ONE

I almost phoned Gary that night. I never phoned him. Until that day out in Glasgow, I didn't think Gary liked me much. Would one day have changed his opinion of me? That's what stopped me in the end. The guy maybe still didn't like me – why would he listen to me or my worries? But he was the only one who seemed actually bothered about this the way I was.

I couldn't phone Baz. I wanted to avoid him, for a couple of days at least. He was never afraid. He'd laugh at my fears.

The next couple of nights I stayed in, wrapped in a duvet, not talking to anyone, hardly eating. I could hear my mother in the living room talking about me.

"I'm worried about him, Vince. Something's wrong with him. A few days ago he's laughing and joking and I think he's fine now, and then... something changes him. And I can't get through to him."

I didn't even listen to his answer. I pulled the duvet right over my head. He was probably suggesting a social worker or, even worse, some kind of psychologist. They'd done it before. One day they would put me into care, I was sure of it.

They didn't have to worry. I wouldn't see the boys again. That's what I decided. I could stay away from them all. I didn't have to see them. They all went to a different school from me. No reason for us ever to get together again. Yes, I would start afresh. No Baz either. Definitely no Baz.

Al Butler's face kept flashing onto the TV screen when I would least expect it.

ALAN BUTLER. KNOWN CRIMINAL. GANGLAND EXECUTION. NO CLUES.

Though nothing linking him to the fire.

Yet I felt better those few days. Lucie and me walking to school together, walking home, talking all the way, and I knew she liked it too. I told her I'd done exactly what she'd suggested, and I could see she was pleased about that. I was even thinking of asking her if she wanted to go to the movies on Saturday night. Not a date. You didn't date girls like Lucie. Just a pal thing.

And after a few days and nothing else happening, I began to relax. I began to think I had been stupid even worrying about it in the first place. Al Butler had made a lot of enemies. His death, his murder, had nothing to do with the fire. And even if it had, Lucie was right. We were only boys. As if gangsters would come after us. It seemed ridiculous now. Baz was right too. There was nothing to be afraid of. Me and Gary were overreacting, dramatising everything.

And then, the dog died.

THIRTY-TWO

It was Gary who called me. "Have you heard from Mickey?" he asked.

I held my breath. Gary's voice was shaking. Something was wrong. "Not seen anybody for a while. Is he all right?"

Gary hesitated. I heard him swallow nervously before he spoke. "His dog died, Logan."

It wasn't what I was expecting, so I laughed. After all we had been through, Mickey was cut up about his dog? I mean, the mutt was ancient. Then I remembered how he had had Ricky since he was three. He took it everywhere. We thought it was a scruffy mongrel of a dog. Mickey didn't. Mickey was always stroking it and clapping it, talking to it as if it was his best friend. He loved that dog, and the dog loved him right back. Nothing to laugh about.

I apologised right away. "Sorry about that. Och, he must be gutted. Did it get run over?" That was my first thought. A lot of dogs wandered free on the estate. Accidents were always happening. But even as I said it I remembered Mickey's dog was kept on a lead, taken for walks, taken care of as if it was a champion at Crufts. It couldn't have been run over. "Was it old age?"

Gary didn't answer for a second. "You're probably the only one I could say this to," he began, "but I don't think it was any kind of an accident. Mickey couldn't find it last night, and you know how he took care of that dog, it was always with him. Slept on his bed and everything. It was gone all night, and then this morning he found it outside his back door, just lying there. Dead." There was another long pause. "It was poisoned, Logan."

"Poisoned...? You think somebody deliberately poisoned it? Who would poison Mickey's dog, Gary? What are you trying to say?"

"His mum's saying it probably wandered off and ate something it shouldn't have. And then found its way back home and died on the doorstep." His words tumbled out in a long unbroken stream.

"You don't think so, do you?"

He answered my question with another question. "You don't think so either, do you?"

"How do you know it was poisoned?"

"Vet cut him up to find out. Said it was rat poison, he must have ate it without thinking." Gary started to whisper as if he thought someone might be listening. "Rat poison. That dog was hardly out of Mickey's sight. Somebody snatched him that night, and poisoned him, and we know who, don't we?" He didn't wait for me to answer. "It was a warning, Logan. A warning."

It was what I was thinking too, but it was a crazy idea. "But, poisoning a dog, Gary? It seems a bit lame for Glasgow gangsters."

"I read they once cut off a dog's head, left it on a billiard table. This guy's favourite dog and he owed them money, and they cut off its head... That was like a warning too."

"Well, they didn't cut off Mickey's dog's head."

"The dog's dead, isn't it?"

I couldn't help thinking he was right. "What does Mickey say?"

"I can't say anything to Mickey," Gary said. "He's so heartbroken, if he thought somebody deliberately poisoned his dog he'd go crazy."

"We could be wrong, Gary," I said.

"I wish I believed that," Gary said. "But I've got a feeling this is only the beginning. Al Butler, and now this."

I had a feeling he was right. That this was only the beginning.

THIRTY-THREE

I called Baz after that. After all my promises to keep away from them all, and here I was, calling Baz. But I had to talk to him, tell him about Mickey's dog. I knew what he would say.

"That's nothing to do with us." So confident of that, he didn't hesitate for a moment.

"You don't think so? Definitely?"

"Somebody's either accidentally poisoned it, or done it deliberately, but it's nothing to do with gangsters. You know what some of the gangs round here are like. Hey! The Young Bow!" I could imagine him snapping his fingers as if he'd just thought of it. "Yeah, the Young Bow. They said they were going to get us, didn't they?

We led them into a trap. If it was anybody, it was them."

The Young Bow! I'd forgotten all about them. I was almost relieved to believe it might have been them.

"But it was left right on his doorstep. Like they wanted him to know it was a warning. Would the Young Bow do that?"

Baz brushed that aside. "Of course they would."

"You really don't think it's a warning from..."

He didn't even let me finish. "Gangsters!" he spat the word out. "No. Don't think that. But listen. Ok, let's say it wasn't the Young Bow, the poor mutt probably just ate something it shouldn't. Happens all the time."

What he said was sensible, and I wanted so much to believe it.

"Come on, Logan, gangsters after us? Do you think they're gonny bother with us? Boys! And these gangsters are so terrifying all they can do is poison a mangy dog... You can't really believe that." He was laughing.

It was stupid, of course it was stupid. I tried to believe it so I'd feel better.

The feeling didn't last long. If I could have phoned Mickey I would have, but Gary was right, it wouldn't be fair telling him our suspicions, that someone had deliberately poisoned his dog. And anyway, Mickey wasn't really any special friend of mine.

I did tell Lucie.

"Aw, who'd be bad enough to kill a little dog?"

She knew exactly who I thought could be bad enough.

"Maybe it was an accident." I said, hopefully, still trying to convince myself.

"Bet it wasn't," she said. "Bet somebody did it deliberately. Not everybody's as nice as us, Logan. But not gangsters. I think your best bet is the Young Bow."

That made me laugh. She was actually agreeing with Baz.

"There's a lot of nasty people going about, Logan. Some of them would have done it."

I so hoped she was right. "Poor Mickey," I said. "He really loved that dog."

I saw Gary and Claude the next night at the precinct. It was a Saturday evening. Baz hadn't turned up where I usually met him, and he didn't answer his phone. Mickey wasn't there either, in mourning for his dog. We were all miserable.

"Taking the grieving process a bit too far, eh?" I suggested. I was trying to lighten the mood, that was all. I wasn't serious.

Claude glared at me. "Mickey loved that dog." His face was grim.

Gary held his arm. "Logan doesn't know Mickey like you do." He glanced at me. "Claude and Mickey been friends forever."

Why did I always say the wrong thing? I wanted to make it up to them. "Sorry. That's me trying to be funny again. Do you think we should go and see him?"

Gary shook his head. "Naw, he just wants to be on his own with his family." Then he added, sounding a bit embarrassed, "Me and Claude, we visited him last night."

Without me. Without even asking me. I was going to ask if Baz was there too, but somehow I knew he hadn't been invited either.

"We didn't say anything about someone doing it deliberately, ok?" Gary said.

I nodded. "Of course not."

"Anyway, it's all a load of old rubbish." Claude spat on the ground. "It'll be the Young Bow, and their furry leader!" he giggled. "Gangsters!" he said. "As if gangsters are going to bother with us."

He began dancing around, doing a made-up rap song, all about gangsters and dead dogs. In the end we were all dancing around the precinct, rapping along with him. Even people passing by were laughing at us.

I felt almost happy as I walked home that night, or rather as I danced home. Still singing to myself, I saw people watching me – must have thought I was soft in the head. But that didn't matter. So a dog was dead. Nasty business poisoning a wee dog. But nothing to do with us, or the fire, or the death of Al Butler. Of course it wasn't. Claude and Baz were right. If it was anybody, it was the Young Bow's sick revenge for leading them into an ambush. As if gangsters would bother with boys like us.

But Claude won't be dancing any more for a long time. That night, on his way home, as he walked down one of the lonely alleys on the estate, Claude was attacked and his legs were broken.

THIRTY-FOUR

Gary called me at lunchtime next day. I was sitting on the sofa, getting stuck into a late breakfast when my phone rang. His voice was shaking. "Claude's in hospital," he told me. "Two broken legs."

I jumped to my feet. My cornflakes went everywhere. "What happened?"

I remember praying he would say it was some kind of accident. Claude had fallen down some stairs. Been hit by a bus. Anything.

His voice rose. "What do you think happened? It was after he left us last night. He's on his way home and he gets jumped. They broke his legs. Two broken legs, do you know what that is?" His voice was getting higher by the minute. "Classic gangster technique. The IRA did it, the gangsters do it." I could picture him on the phone, breathing hard, bouncing about on the balls of his feet the way he always did when he was nervous.

"Did Claude tell you that?"

"I've not seen him. But what else could it be? Al Butler, Mickey's dog, and now this. No way this is the Young Bow. They're just boys as well, they wouldn't do a thing like this. This is Mad Mike – the Machans! They're after us. They're definitely picking us off one by one."

But, now I'd had time to take it in, I was doubtful. "Come on, Gary, don't let's jump to conclusions. How did you find out?"

I could hear his nervous swallow. "Claude's auntie," he said. "She phoned my mum."

"So you don't really know how it happened? You're just speculating?"

I could almost see him nodding his head, thinking about that. "Ok, I see what you mean, it could have been anybody... But it's too much of a coincidence."

"Let's wait till we see Claude. Are you going to the hospital?"

"I'm going at visiting tonight... Are you going to come with me?"

He wanted company. And I needed to see Claude too. I was so glad he asked me. "Yeah, of course I'm coming."

THIRTY-FIVE

It was just me and Gary who went to the hospital. Baz didn't come. I did call him, but he said hospitals and him didn't agree. His dad had died in one, he said, almost laughing. I was glad he didn't come. I knew Gary was too. We talked more freely when Baz wasn't there.

We took a bus to the hospital and Gary couldn't stop talking about what had happened to Claude. His voice trembled with his every word.

"You're really scared, Gary," I said.

"Do you blame me? Claude's lying in hospital. Al Butler's dead. So's Mickey's dog. Yeah, sure I'm scared."

"We've got to wait and see what Claude says." There could be so many other reasons for Claude being attacked.

163

I kept thinking about the Young Bow. It must have been them. They had told us they would get us, hadn't they? I wanted so much for them to be responsible.

Visiting hadn't started when we arrived. People were standing about, waiting for the ward doors to open, and I saw Claude's mum sitting right outside the ward – any closer and she would have been inside. I had only seen her once – the night we'd been taken home by the police – but who could forget her? She was a big woman with a high-pitched voice that could stop traffic at fifty yards. And a drama queen reaction to everything. She caught sight of us and came to life. She leapt from the seat and rushed down the corridor with her coat flying behind her. She looked like an oversized bat.

"You! I blame you! A bad influence. My Claude was never in trouble till he took up with you!"

We were so taken aback we didn't even step back. We never stood a chance. She lifted her handbag and walloped Gary over the head. He tried to cover his head with his hands, but he was too late.

"Mrs Handley—" I tried to avoid her, but she didn't miss me either. She slammed the bag against my shoulder.

Her finger was inches from my face. "This has all happened since you turned up. You keep away from him. Hear me?"

I knew my face was bright red. I was trying hard to understand. Why was she blaming me for everything?

Claude's sister, Taylor, came running behind her

mum. She was a real looker with huge dark eyes; she pulled her mother away. But she was protecting her mother, not us. Those huge eyes were icy cold as she glared in our direction.

"We don't even know what happened to Claude." I told them.

"It was after he left us." Gary said. "Nothing to do with us."

And then at the same time we both asked. "What *did* happen to Claude?"

Just then, the ward doors opened, so we didn't get an answer. Visiting hour had begun. Mrs Handley pushed us back roughly. "You're not coming in! Go away!"

Gary and I just stood looking at each other, not knowing what to do. Taylor led her mum to the doors but then slipped back. "She's really upset. Look, just wait. You can go in when we're finished. Only don't let Mum see you."

"How did it happen, Taylor?" Gary asked her.

She shook her head. "Don't know. We didn't even hear about it till the middle of the night. My mum was going crazy 'cos he hadn't come in. Then we got a phone call to say that someone had found him on the street, phoned an ambulance. He just says somebody attacked him. But he doesn't know who." She glanced toward the ward. "Look, I better go."

So we sat in the corridor, not knowing what to say to each other.

"I thought the cops would be here," Gary said eventually. He looked round as if he was expecting one to pop up between the seats.

"Been and gone probably."

"Will they want to talk to us, do you think?"

We both knew they would. It alarmed Gary. It alarmed me too. Gary was so nervous, goodness knows what he might tell them.

He leaned forward, put his head in his hands. "The Machans – they must know who we are. They must be watching us and they're coming after us, one by one." His voice was a mumble. "And it will be even worse if they know the police have interviewed us."

But I had an answer for that. "It won't matter if the polis do interview us, Gary," I said "This attack happened after Claude left us. We haven't got anything to tell them."

He was suddenly shouting: "We're his mates! They'll ask if we might know who did this. And we don't dare tell them anything... Or goodness knows what will happen to us." A couple of people waiting in the corridor turned to look at us. I touched his arm to quieten him.

"But we *don't* know anything, Gary, and that's all we are gonny tell the polis." I reminded him, "You're jumping to conclusions."

We had to wait for almost the full hour before Claude's mum and his sister came out. And then do you know what we did? We hid. We squeezed in behind a snack machine and hoped his mum wouldn't spot us. Didn't want walloped with that handbag again. Claude's mum's eyes were puffy with tears. She held a hanky to her face. Didn't even look our way. Taylor did. She let her mother take a few steps ahead and then she came back to us. "You've got a couple of minutes. See if he'll talk to you."

"How is he?"

She looked at me as if I was mad. "He's got two broken legs. He's brilliant. What do you think?"

I held her back. "Whatever happened to Claude, it was nothing to do with us." I was trying to reassure myself as much as her.

She snatched her arm away. "Wasn't it? He says he didn't see who attacked him. I think he's lying. He knows. See if you can get any more out of him."

Then she was off, running after her crying mother.

THIRTY-SIX

Claude was in the last bed, by the window. He was lying flat on his back with his plastered legs raised on two white pillows. Any other time we would have made a joke of that, had a laugh about it. Nobody laughed now.

All I could see was the side of his face, but Claude looked sick. His skin had a waxy greyness to it. He was turned away from us, staring out of the window. I wondered what he was thinking.

Gary ran round to the other side of the bed. He waved his arms, trying to make his mate smile. "Hi Claude." Claude wasn't smiling. "What happened, Claude? Your sister said you never saw who did it," Gary looked at

Claude hopefully. "Is that right, Claude? You don't know who did it?"

"Was it the Young Bow?" I asked him, wanting a 'yes'. Desperate for a 'yes'.

It took Claude a moment to answer us, and when he did, he didn't turn to me. He didn't even look at Gary, just kept staring out of the window. His voice was only a whisper, as if he was afraid someone might be listening. He didn't even swear – that was a really bad sign.

"I told the police I didn't see who did it, told them I didn't have a clue why anybody would do this to me... That's what I told them. But that was a lie." He let out a long sigh. Gary flopped onto the seat by Claude's bed, but Claude just kept whispering to the window. "This guy," he went on. "This guy, he just came out of the dark behind me. I thought he wanted past. I moved to let him go by me and he slammed me up against the wall. That's when I saw there was two of them. One on either side of me. I tried to turn round to see who the second guy was, but the first guy just grabbed me and threw me down. He was all dressed in black, like a ninja. Then I saw a baseball bat coming down on my legs." His voice shook with the memory. "I passed out."

"Was it someone from the Young Bow? Had to be," Gary asked.

At last Claude turned and I saw his face, drained of colour, still looking frightened. "No, it wasn't anybody from the Young Bow. One of them said something just before he hit me. He bent down and he said, 'Take your medicine like a man, little boy, and pass on a message to your friends: *Nobody messes with us. We're coming for the lot of you.*'"

The blood in my veins went ice cold.

Claude blinked back tears. "Know what else he said to me? He said, 'And when the cops ask, you don't know who did this. Ok? You or your friends say a word, and we'll make it even worse for you.'" His voice broke then. He looked from me to Gary. "So promise you won't tell anybody what I said. *Promise!*" His voice was a whisper and a scream all at the same time. "They're not finished. They're coming after you as well."

THIRTY-SEVEN

We left the ward in a daze. "They're coming for us." Gary's voice was a whisper. "That's what he said. They'll get the lot of us." I held his arm, felt it tremble under my fingers. "You heard what Claude said. They're going to get us all. And we *cannot* tell anybody that."

I knew he was right. "Well, if we've got to tell the police anything, we can say we think it was the Young Bow."

If I'd hit him with a brick he couldn't have looked more shocked. "Do you know nothing, Logan? We can't grass up the Young Bow!"

"So we just don't tell the cops anything? Is that what you're saying?"

Gary shook his head. "It's as if these gangsters know us. Know everything about us. They knew Mickey loved his dog. They knew where they could find Claude, the way he walked home. They know about us all."

"All this because we were there when their warehouse was torched? I don't understand. They got Al Butler. Why come after us?"

Gary shook his head. "We messed with their property. Nobody does that to the Machans, Logan. And I heard my dad and my uncle talking: they said there would have been more in that warehouse than just carpets. It would be a cover for something else, drugs probably. Remember Al Butler patting his pockets, talking about his stash? He stole drugs from them, and they might think we did as well. And as if that's not bad enough, we sent the whole place up in flames. They're gonny teach us all a lesson. Take our medicine. And they know we can't say anything, because if we do, it's not just us that might suffer. They might go after our families as well."

"We've got enough to deal with without worrying about that, too."

I said it to make him feel better, that was all. He didn't take it that way.

He turned on me. "You wouldn't worry about your family anyway, would you? You've got no time for your mum, or her man. I mean... what do you care about, Logan? Eh, *who* do you care about? Nobody, as far as I can tell." He was sorry he said it almost as soon as the words were out. He pushed his fist against his mouth as if he could stuff the words back in. "Sorry. I shouldn't have said that. I'm just so scared, and if anything happened to my family because of me..." He shook his head. "I'd rather be dead."

His words hurt more than I can tell you. But why shouldn't he believe that? I was always talking about my mum, always talking about Vince. Never saying anything good about them. Never mentioned all the good things my mum did for me. Was that why he thought that I didn't care about her, about anyone? Did the other boys think that about me too? That I cared about no one? I must seem like a right scumbag to them.

Gary left me as soon as we came out of the hospital. Running for his bus, not waiting for me, with hardly a "Goodnight." He wanted away from me. He wanted the safety of home.

"We better not see each other for a while," was all he said before he was off.

"Call me if the cops visit you!" I shouted after him. I didn't know if he would or not. Don't even know if he heard me. Gary was scared. I was scared too. Scared of what he would say if he did talk to them. Phrases like 'loose cannon' and 'weakest link' came to mind.

I called Baz on the way home. "You should have come to see Claude," I said.

"Don't like hospitals," he said. No apology. Baz never apologised. "Did he say who did it?"

"A couple of guys in black came after him on the way home." I was dying to tell him what Claude had told us, "But wait, Baz, wait till you hear what they said to Claude..." I didn't get finished. He cut me off, dismissed it. I could imagine him flicking his hand as if he was brushing away a fly.

"Don't want to hear anything about it. I tell you, it'll be the Young Bow. We should get them for this. We could go over there tomorrow night. Face them. Confront them."

It was the last thing I wanted, and I was sure it would be the worst thing to do. "No! I think we should keep a low profile. The polis will probably be interviewing all of us."

"Yeah, well, ok," he said reluctantly. "But, see when this is over, we are going to get right into that crowd."

"I know, definitely," I said quickly, glad he was at least pushing aside the idea of another confrontation for the moment. "I'm just worried about Gary, he's dead scared. I've never seen him like this."

"Scared enough to grass on us?"

"Naw! Naw!" I blurted it out. I was afraid of Baz's reaction if Gary did grass. "Gary's no grass. You said that yourself."

"I sometimes think I don't know the boys at all, Logan," Baz said. "I know you. I trust you."

I felt my heart lift when he said that. Baz trusted me. The other boys thought I had no feelings for anyone. But not Baz. He knew me. I never wanted to let him down. "You can depend on me, Baz," I said.

I imagined him nodding, agreeing with me. "Hey Logan, let's face it, the cops are coming. We've just gotta keep our heads. Get our stories straight. Ok?"

I wasn't so scared when I spoke to him. I could draw my courage from him.

I switched off the phone and hurried home.

There had been something else scaring me that I didn't dare put into words. I had been thinking about it since Gary had left me.

First Al Butler dies, then Mickey's dog, and now Claude. Who had been first into that warehouse the night of the fire? I re-ran the scene in my head. It had been Al Butler. I remembered him, turning his face to the cameras, daring them to see him. Then Mickey had run in. And then Claude. I remember how he fell back over one of the boxes and we all laughed. And that was the sequence they had been attacked. Al Butler, then Mickey and now Claude.

Gary had run inside next. I could see it all as if I was watching the rerun of an old film. Gary was next, then finally me – and Baz almost at the same time.

Was I making all this up? I didn't know any more. But if anything happened to Gary... Then I'd be sure I was right.

THIRTY-EIGHT

The next day at school, Lucie knew all about Claude. How did she always find out these things? His story hadn't hit any papers. Word travels fast on the streets, I suppose.

"So what happened to him?"

I wasn't going to tell her what Claude had told us. Saying it out loud would make it true somehow. Sharing it with someone outside our circle just wouldn't be the sensible thing to do. Maybe I had told Lucie too much already. Couldn't risk putting her in any more danger. I just shrugged. "Random attack. He was at the wrong place at the wrong time."

"Sure about that?" she said, as if she didn't believe me.

176

"What else could it be?"

She didn't answer that. She changed the subject. "Cops been to talk to you?"

"No. Have they come to talk to you?"

That made her laugh. Her face changed completely when she laughed. Dimples appeared on her cheeks, her small white teeth seemed to shine. She should laugh more often. "And why would anybody want to interview me?"

"You're like that Miss blinking Marple. Always asking questions."

"And never getting any answers," she said, smiling. "Not from you anyway."

"It happened after we left him, Lucie. I couldn't tell them anything. But I suppose you're right. The police will come."

Sure enough, two policemen were waiting for me in the house when I went home. To make things worse, my mother wasn't there. Only Vince. They all stood up when I went in to the living room. First time I noticed how tall Vince was. As tall as the two cops standing beside him.

"It's about Claude," Vince said.

I didn't sit down.

The two policemen introduced themselves. Then they sat down again. They seemed to be studying my face. It was Vince who spoke first: "Sit down, Logan."

Don't normally do what he tells me, but I sat down

on the sofa beside him. Now I was face to face with the officers. It was as if they were waiting for me to speak. I tried to stay silent, but I know I looked nervous.

"Ok, who's the good cop and who's the bad cop?" I tried to sound funny. Don't think it worked.

Neither of them smiled. Vince tutted, annoyed at me.

"So, this is about Claude?" I said.

"Do you know what happened to him?"

"He doesn't know who did it," I said. "That's what he told us."

The younger one took out a notebook and began writing down what I said.

"That's what he's saying," the other one said, "but the boy's scared. We think maybe he does know."

"I was at the hospital last night. I saw him. He doesn't know who did it," I began to rattle on. As soon as I started talking, it was like a cork coming out of a bottle – everything came pouring out. "He says he never saw who did it, could have been anybody. Just somebody in black. There's loads of gangs around here. Had to be one of them." I was careful not to mention the Young Bow, but that was the first thing the policeman picked up on.

"You're saying it could be that gang you had the trouble with a couple of weeks ago?"

It was the last thing I wanted them to think. "No! No! I didn't mean that."

"We will be questioning them anyway," he said.

"Don't tell them I said it was them. I'm not saying that." I know I sounded panicky but I couldn't help it. I remembered what Gary had said about grassing. I didn't care about the Young Bow or what they might think of me. But all at once, in that moment, I realised I didn't want to let Gary down.

The policeman shook his head. "No. We won't mention you. Don't worry about that."

After that they said nothing, as if they were waiting for me to tell them more. "Oh come on, you know there's always trouble here. I don't get what you expect me to know anyway," I tried for a laugh. "I mean, you're making me feel guilty here."

"*Are* you guilty of something?" the younger one said.

Honest, you could have knocked me over right then. What was he saying that for? Did they know about the trouble I'd got into in Aberdeen? What were they trying to make me say? "Me? I didn't do anything. Claude's my mate. He didn't say it was me, did he?"

The boys didn't like me – that thought wound through my mind like a snake... They only tolerated me because of Baz.

"No," I was told after a long pause. "Of course we don't think you're a suspect. Claude isn't saying too much actually. We know he's hiding something. He knows more than he's telling. We're trying to protect him here. Trying to protect you all. We're trying to find out who did it. If you know anything you should tell us."

"No! He never saw who did it. That's what he told us."

"You tell the truth now!" Vince snapped at me. He got to his feet, towering above me. "If Claude's told you who did it, you speak up. It's for your own good."

I flinched away from him. I hoped that would make the cops think I was expecting him to hit me, was used to it.

"I don't know who did it." Did I shout? I might have. I looked back to the policemen. "If I knew I would tell you. Claude's my mate. He didn't tell us anything either."

I had to go over everything that had happened the night Claude was attacked. There was nothing I could tell but the truth, and it's funny how relaxed you feel when you know you are telling the truth.

Finally they left saying I was to contact them if I found out anything more, and that they might be back with more questions.

As soon as they'd gone, Vince turned on me. "They'll be back, don't doubt it. They know you were lying. I know you were lying. You know who did this to your mate."

"I suppose you took great pleasure in telling them all the trouble I got into in Aberdeen."

"No. I didn't tell them. But only for your mother's sake, not for yours."

He held me back as I tried to leave the room. "Logan. Tell me what's wrong. Your mum and I both know you're worried about something. Tell me; I want to help you."

What a joke! "YOU! You can't even help yourself."

And I pulled away from him and ran out of the room.

THIRTY-NINE

I went out to the walkway to call Baz. I wanted to warn him, prepare him for what the police would ask.

"I've had them here too," he said. Different cops, same questions.

But they hadn't suggested to him that he might have been the one who did it.

"They're winding you up, mate," he said when I told him that. "Trying to trick you. Hoping you would tell them something they didn't know. They did the same with me."

"They didn't accuse you of attacking Claude?"

"No. But they asked me what other gangs I was in. What I was doing that night. I wasn't there, remember?

And all the other stuff they asked you, they asked me too."

I phoned Gary first thing next morning. I seemed to be calling him more with each passing day. The police had been to see him too – probably, by the way he described them, the same cops who had visited me.

"Did you tell them anything?" Gary was the weakest link. Maybe he had blabbed everything to the cops.

"Of course I didn't." He snapped at me. "What do you think I am? I never said nothing."

"Ok, ok, keep your hair on."

I knew I couldn't tell Gary about my suspicions that we were being taken out in sequence. He'd freak out. Instead I tried to make him laugh.

"I don't suppose they'd accept an apology – a nice card saying, 'Dear Mad Mike, sorry we torched your warehouse. We include a gift card from Tesco as compensation.'"

To my surprise, Gary laughed. "You can be so funny at times, Logan. I wish it as was simple as that." Then his voice became a whisper. As if he was afraid someone might be listening. "No chance. They're not gonny stop till they get us."

The story of Claude's attack was in the papers. Only a small item, about a boy attacked in an alley on the estate. Not major news with all the other terrible things happening in the world. After I read it, I tried to call Baz. I tried to call Gary. No answer from either of them. I felt alone.

Of course Vince had told my mother about the police visit. "I had to tell her, Logan," he told me. He sounded sincere, I have to give him that. "The neighbours saw the police come in here. Of course I had to tell her."

"It was about Claude."

But she wouldn't listen.

"Do you know who did it, Logan? Because if you do, you've got to tell them."

To my surprise it was Vince who came to my rescue. "I said that too, Marie, but I've thought about it, and you've got to understand how the boy feels. He can't grass. Even if he knows, he can't grass." Then he looked at me. "But I wish you would tell *us*, Logan."

Mum flopped on the sofa. "I thought it would be different here. All the trouble you got into in Aberdeen, I thought it would stop down here."

She talked as if I'd been some kind of major criminal in Aberdeen. I'd only got in with the wrong crowd. Easily led. Lucie's words bounded back at me. I'd been told that before somewhere. But where? I couldn't think.

When I came back into the house that evening, Mum was just hanging up the phone. She looked as if she'd been crying. "That was Claude's mum," she said.

Claude's mum had never called our house before. My heart sank. "Has anything else happened to him?"

"She's warning me that you better keep well back from her son. You're a bad influence, she says. I thought she was going to come through the phone at me."

"Me! *I'm* a bad influence!" I almost said she'd better have phoned the other boys' parents too. Especially Gary's and Baz's. Gary with his wide boy father, and Baz, who was the one who had egged us on to run in after Al Butler. He was the one who had dared him to set the place alight. Yet I didn't mention their names. Couldn't bring them into it, even then. But it wasn't fair, Claude's mum calling here. I was the least bad influence in the gang.

"Why is she blaming you, Logan?"

"Because I always seem to get the blame for everything that happens."

I stormed into my room. I so wanted someone to talk to. But no matter how often I texted or rang, no replies – not from Gary, not from Baz.

I was stuck with Lucie, and there was only so much I could tell her. Swerving round the truth. But I had to talk to someone, and next day at school I did tell her what Claude's mum had said. That had hurt.

"Imagine, blaming me! Blame everybody else but her son, I suppose."

"Yeah," Lucie said. "Take responsibility for your own actions, don't blame other people."

"You always do, don't you, Lucie?"

"So should you. Don't blame anyone else. It's you."

She was right, of course. In my head, though I would never say it to anyone else, in my head I know I was beginning to blame Baz. I did too much to please him, to keep him happy. But then, I had had a choice. I shouldn't have listened to him, and I had. Lucie was right. It was me who was responsible.

"Somebody is after us, Lucie. But I don't want you involved, or my mum. I don't want to put you in any danger."

Lucie touched my arm. Lucie never touched me, so she took me by surprise. "You're a really nice boy, Logan. You are so much better without..." she hesitated. "By yourself. Just be yourself. Please."

Without Baz, that's what she was going to say. Perhaps he had been given the same advice about me. That he was better without me. Perhaps that's why he wasn't answering my texts. I tried again later and still no answer. He didn't text me back. Neither did Gary.

I told myself we were all trying to keep back from each other. We were all scared.

But I had to know what was happening. So after school next day I didn't wait for Lucie. Instead, I took a detour and went to Gary's house. I'd had a bad feeling in my stomach all that day. And I knew as soon as the door was opened that something was wrong.

A man was standing there. I didn't know him, but he

turned out to be Gary's uncle. "Do you know where he is?" First thing he said, his voice brusque.

Then he gripped my arm and pulled me into the house. "It's that boy Gary runs around with," he was saying as he led me into the living room. Not 'his friend', or 'his mate'. Just 'that boy he runs around with'.

Gary's mum stood up as I came in. She didn't look so pretty now. Her eyes were puffy, her face was streaked with tears. "You know where he is?" A question? A statement? She sounded desperate. Hopeful too, that I might know something. She grabbed my shoulders. "If you know where he is, please tell us."

A big man appeared from one of the rooms. Gary's dad. I'd met him before a few times when he'd picked up Gary from the precinct. "Do you know where Gary's gone?"

I didn't want to hear what they were telling me. "What do you mean? Gary's gone?"

His dad's face was grim with worry. "We haven't seen Gary since yesterday."

FORTY

They didn't ask me to sit down. In fact, now that she saw I knew nothing, Gary's mum just glared at me. As if she was blaming me too. I looked from her angry gaze to her husband's. He looked more worried than angry. Every time I had seen him before, he always had a cheery smile on his face. He was one of those men everyone seemed to like, selling stuff on the cheap, always a bit on the dodgy side, but no one had a bad word for him even though they knew he was a bit of a crook.

He wasn't smiling now.

"He was shaking like a leaf when he came home from that hospital," he said. It was as if he had repeated that same thing over and over. "He wouldn't tell us why."

He took a threatening step toward me. "So you tell me, what happened at the hospital? Who attacked Claude?"

"Claude doesn't know who attacked him. His mother thinks we know, but we don't." The lies all tumbled out quickly because how could I tell the truth? That Mad Mike Machan might have sent his enforcers after us because we'd been there when his property was torched? It would only get us all into more trouble – trouble with the Machans, and it sounded too unbelievable, and anyway, telling the truth would lead to too many other questions.

Gary's dad might be a bit of a crook, but he had never been arrested, and never been involved in any violence. If Gary hadn't told him anything, how could I? Gary wouldn't want me to tell him anything.

"We were scared whoever did it would come after us too. Because we were mates."

I said it as if it was true. I almost believed it myself. A band of mindless Nazi thugs roaming the estate were coming after us. It sounded true. "That's all I know. I'm scared too."

His dad sat on the sofa next to his wife.

"How long's he been gone?" I asked.

His dad's voice was lifeless. "Went off to school yesterday. Didn't get there. Don't know where he's gone. Been on to cousins, uncles, as many people as we can think of."

"He's been gone before, bruv," the uncle said. He

looked like the ugly version of Gary's dad. As if when they'd been handing out the good looks in the family he'd been at the back of the queue. "You know our Gary. One argument and he's away." He was trying to make a joke of it.

His brother looked up at him. "We didn't have an argument. I mean, not this time." Then his tone softened. "I know, you're only trying to make us feel better. Thanks bruv."

"What do the police say?" Had to ask, though I didn't want to.

"They're not taking it seriously. He's not been gone long enough and this isn't the first time he's run off." Gary had run away before, I remembered him telling us that. He always came back. Safe and sound. That thought made me feel better.

"He'll come back," I said it almost to myself.

"Yeah, yeah, he'll come back." His dad was trying to reassure himself, and his wife. She began to sob quietly and he put his arms round her and drew her to him. "Don't cry, darlin'. Our boy will be ok. He can take care of himself."

In answer she clutched at his hand, and he kissed her brow. I watched, amazed. I never saw tenderness like that in my house. Not any more. *How on earth could Gary run away from here?* I thought. There was love in this house. Love for him, and his parents had love for each other. It hurt to realise I was jealous.

I left Gary's and just had to talk to Baz. If he didn't answer his phone this time, I was going to his house, I decided.

He answered on the first ring. "Where have you been? I was beginning to think you'd run off with Gary."

He hesitated. "Gary's gone?"

"Just been to his house. His family's cracking up. The cops'll be back asking us about this now as well."

"Yeah, they will."

"Do you think we should tell them?"

"Tell them what?" Baz shouted down the phone at me. "We don't know anything. Gary's run away before. He'll come back. You wait and see."

It was only after I'd come off the phone I realised he hadn't answered my question. I still didn't know where he'd been.

That night, those same two policemen came back to the house. This time my mum was there.

"You have absolutely no idea why Gary would go on the run?"

I sat beside Mum on the couch. Shook my head. "No." I said.

"Was he afraid of something?"

I shrugged my shoulders. "Well, those guys that attacked Claude, he was scared they might come back for us. We're his mates. That's the only reason I can think of."

"Has he been in touch with you?"

I shook my head. "I've tried phoning him, but... there's no answer."

"Was he being bullied by anyone, maybe at school?" The sudden change of direction in his questions took me by surprise. A lot of kids do run away if they're being bullied, don't they?

"He might have been." I nodded. "I wasn't in his school. You should ask his pals at that school."

One of the policemen leaned across to me. "You look relieved about that."

Did my face go red? It might have.

"I know he was worried that the gang that attacked Claude would come and get him, really worried about that." How often did I have to say it to them?

"Do you really think that's why he ran away?"

"I'm not the detective," I said. Mum poked me in the ribs. The policeman scowled. "Anyway, he'll come back. He's run away before. He always comes back." I so wanted that to be true.

As soon as they left the house, Mum grabbed my hand. "Do you know anything about that boy running away?"

"No."

"Because if you know where he is, if you've heard from him, you should tell the police. Please, tell the police. You wouldn't be grassing anybody up. You're hiding something. They can see it. I can see it. What is it, Logan? I only want to help you, son."

And if I told her? Would they come after her too? I only wanted to protect her, but I couldn't let her see that. So, I reacted like a hooligan. I pulled my hand away from hers. "Why won't you believe me? I don't know anything. I wish I knew where he is, but I don't."

She was on the verge of tears. "I know you think everything would be great if we moved back to Aberdeen, if Vince wasn't here," she said. "But we had to get away from Aberdeen, and Vince is a good man if you give him a chance. I'm so afraid for you, Logan."

"You don't have to worry about me."

I slammed out of the house before she could stop me.

There was only one person I could talk to about this, and it was Baz. He was the only one left for me.

I called him as soon as I was outside. The police had already been to him too.

"We've just got to keep our heads down. Gary'll come back." But he didn't sound so sure now.

I wish, I thought then, *I wish I was anywhere else but here.*

FORTY-ONE

Gary didn't come back. Not the next day, nor the next. I was afraid to call his house, and though there was an item about him in the local rag, read by about fifty people on the estate, he didn't make the national news. Too many teenagers running away, going missing, for his disappearance to be either unusual or interesting. But in the local paper there was a CCTV image of him in a shop on the morning he disappeared. He'd stopped on his way to school to buy crisps and coke.

Getting ready for a journey? the paper suggested. Didn't seem to occur to them he might be buying them instead of a canteen dinner at school.

Lucie saw my fear. "That mate of yours still missing?"

she asked one day on our way to school. I had started trying to leave earlier so I would miss her. But that day she caught up with me.

"He's done it before," I said.

"Bit rotten doing that to your family."

"Maybe he's got his reasons," I said.

"He's got a nice family. My mum knows his dad. Bit of a lad, she says, but a good heart."

I looked at her. "A good heart? What's that supposed to mean?"

"It means he helps people. People who can't afford things, he helps them to get them."

"The moneylenders round here help people too. Then they break your legs if you can't pay them back."

"Isn't that what happened to your friend, Claude? Didn't someone break his legs? Did he owe people money? Get on the wrong side of someone?" I would have walked away from her but she held me back. "If you're so scared, why don't you tell the police?"

"You know why," I said.

"Better getting into trouble with them, than with the gangsters don't you think? Eh?"

Thing was, I felt as if I was cracking up. I lay in bed at night and every noise was a threat. The window rattled in the wind and I imagined a black-clothed ninja leaping in, prowling around the house, heading for my room. I imagined my mum getting up to see what the noise was and if she got in his way... he would kill her too. I didn't want anything bad to happen to my mum.

Kill?

Why was I thinking *kill*?

Because they had killed Al Butler, hadn't they?

But he was older, a known criminal; we were just boys. Was that why they had only poisoned Mickey's dog? Was that why they had only broken Claude's legs? *Only?* I drew my own legs up, hugged them, as if I could protect them from this imaginary attacker.

And Gary... Had he simply run away, had they threatened him too... or had they dragged him off into the shadows one night? No, they wouldn't have killed him, would they?

If only I could get in touch with him. Or hear from him. I had tried his mobile from that very first day, but it was dead.

Dead.

Another squeak on the floorboards. Was that a footstep in the hall? Every time I thought I might drift off to sleep another sound would stab me awake.

Next morning I was up and out of the house earlier than usual. I phoned Baz as soon as I hit the walkway. "Are you as jumpy as I am?" I waited for him to say I was being stupid. Big bold Baz would never be afraid like me. There was a long pause.

"I thought someone was following me last night," he said.

"Where? When?"

"Went to the shops, on the way back, heard footsteps. Couldn't see no one, but there was definitely somebody there. And when I began to run, so did he. I just made it home in time."

"Who says we go to the cops, Baz?"

Right away his tone changed. "No! There was no one after me, Logan. It was all my imagination. We're too jumpy that's all. Don't you mention the cops again, ok?"

I spent that day just walking, trying to think. Can't even remember exactly where I went. I couldn't get the thought of someone following Baz out of my mind. I kept glancing round, sure there was a figure behind me, that the footsteps at my back had been there all day, close behind my own. I was suspicious of the least sound. Maybe that was why what happened, happened.

I had only turned into the alley leading to our flats when I saw the shadow. Someone was standing under the stairs where the rubbish chute was, hiding, as if they were waiting for me. I didn't wait to find out who it was. I began to run. A second later that someone was after me. Not my imagination this time. I leapt the wall between the two blocks without looking behind me. I could hear nothing, but I knew the person closing in behind me was still there. The only sound was my own heavy breathing, my own footsteps. I felt as if a panicked rabbit was running inside my chest, my heart was beating so fast. But I was almost home. If I could make the far end of the block, I could race up the stairs and on to my own walkway.

The place seemed quiet, dead almost.

Where was everyone? Usually there were people milling about on the balconies, chatting in doorways. Especially in summer. Now there was no one, just me and this silent stranger right on my tail. Had the neighbours been warned? Something was going to happen. 'Stay indoors, don't be a witness?' It had happened before, attacks in broad daylight. No witnesses. It was how it worked round here.

I searched in my pocket for my key as I ran. I belted around a corner and took the chance to glance at my back. Only a shadow, that was all I saw, all I needed to see. He was still behind me, whoever *he* was. I took the stairs leading to my walkway two at a time. Now I was sure I could hear footsteps, clanging on steel. Speeding up when I did. Footsteps coming closer. But I was well ahead. I could still make it. I dared another glance back. A black shape seemed to loom at the top of the stairs. I couldn't make out anything else, and didn't waste time looking harder. I was almost at my door. My hands shook, the keys jingled. *Don't let me drop them*, I prayed. I fumbled for the lock, couldn't get the key in. It was like a scene from some old movie, or some bad dream. I just couldn't seem to fit the key in the lock. The footsteps were coming closer and closer.

I felt as if I was ready to scream.

FORTY-TWO

The door was hauled open. "What the heck's wrong with you?" It was Vince, and for once I was so glad to see him. I fell inside the house.

"Was somebody after you?" Vince almost lifted me from the floor. "Were you being chased?"

He stepped out of the front door. I held my breath waiting for a fist, or a baseball bat to swing against his face. "There's nobody there," he said.

He closed the door. I stumbled into the living room, flopped onto the sofa, still half expecting someone to kick in the front door and come flying into the flat.

"Must have been my imagination," I said. But it wasn't, was it? Someone *had* been after me, just like they had been after Baz.

"I wish you would tell us what's going on. Me and your mum, we're worried sick about you." His voice was soft. He sounded as if he genuinely cared. I said nothing. "Logan, are the boys that attacked Claude after you?"

"Nothing's going on. I thought somebody was chasing me. It was probably my imagination."

"The somebody that attacked Claude?"

"We don't know who attacked Claude."

"Was someone after Gary, is that why he scarpered? If you know anything, we could go to the police. I'd go with you. You would get protection if that's what you're scared of."

He was still thinking it was another gang after us. Just another gang on the estate. He didn't know how bad it was. The Machans after me, and I go to the police? They'd be bound to find out. They'd warned Claude we were to say nothing. They'd find out I was the one who'd grassed. Another reason to come after me. Or after Mum. Oh yeah, that would be a good plan. I'd never be free of them. Never.

So again, I said nothing. Not because I didn't want to. Because I didn't know what to say.

Vince sat down in the chair across from me. He leaned forward as if he had something real important to say. "Logan? You know your mother's worried about you. She thinks you need someone to talk to... a professional.

Would you talk to them, Logan? Maybe you could tell them what you can't tell us."

I felt my whole body stiffen. A professional. I knew it was coming to this. Then they could put me away somewhere, forget about me. And it would be just her and Vince. I felt sick at the thought of it.

He waited, he must have thought that would make me talk, but I still said nothing. I stared past him, as if I was in another world. In a way, I was. Another scary world. Between the devil and the deep blue sea.

"Logan?" he asked again, and still I didn't answer. He gave up eventually, turning back to the television with a resigned sigh, and I stood up and went into my room, pulled out my phone and called Baz. He was the one I wanted to talk to. I told him everything that had happened.

"Just the way it happened with you," I said.

"Maybe too much like the way it happened with me."

"What do you mean by that?"

"You never actually saw anybody, Logan. Maybe because there was nobody there." He laughed. "You do have some imagination, you know?"

"There was somebody there. It wasn't my imagination." I didn't want him to think that.

"Shouldn't have told you somebody came after me," Baz said. "That might just have made you think somebody was after you too. Might have been somebody innocent, a neighbour. Your imagination would do the rest."

"It wasn't my imagination!" I almost shouted it down the phone.

"Ok, keep your hair on," he said. Then he added. "I believe you."

"You know what I think, Baz? I think maybe Gary isn't coming back, that's what I think. He's not coming back because he can't." It was the first time I had put it into words. "What are we going to do, Baz?"

He didn't answer for a while. "Let's get the hell out of here. Nobody's gonny miss us."

He had plucked the idea out of my own mind. It was what I had been thinking, but I'd been too afraid to actually say it aloud. He was right. And what Vince had said had frightened me. They were going to get someone to talk to me. Someone to get into my mind, my deepest thoughts. I didn't want that. And then they'd put me into care. If I was going to leave, it would me my decision, not theirs. Anyway, I was maybe putting them in real danger just being here. My mum was sick of me, and Vince would be glad to see the back of me. They could play happy families when I was gone from here.

This was the answer to everything.

"I just don't know where we could go," Baz said. Unsure for once. And for once, I felt I was in charge.

"I know where we could go. Aberdeen. We'll go back to Aberdeen. I've got friends there. They'll hide us, look after us."

There was a rap on the door. I closed over the phone.

It was Vince. "Are you talking to yourself again?"

"I was saying my prayers," I said.

Baz was right. We had to get away from here. By this time tomorrow, I would be gone.

FORTY-THREE

I phoned Baz first thing in the morning. I'd hardly slept, awake most of the night working out what we would do. "We'll have to go to school," I told him, in charge for a change. I couldn't miss school, if I didn't turn up they would get in touch with my mum right away. They had to do that if I wasn't there. It was that kind of school. "But we'll meet up later. My mum's working. A double shift. So I won't be missed for ages." He was up for it too. So we made our decision. We would leave that evening. "Unless Gary comes back," I said. If he came back we would stay, find out what had happened to him. You don't know how I hoped he would come back. I even asked Mum to phone his house before I left for school, just to find out.

"You're really worried about him, aren't you?"

What did she want me to say? I hesitated. "Naw, still think he's hopped it. Had an argument with his dad, he's always having arguments with his dad. Why should I worry about him? He never worries about me."

I'd said the wrong thing obviously. She looked disappointed.

"I thought you liked Gary." She said it as if I was a stranger, as if she didn't know me. You know, I think if she hadn't said that, I might have changed my mind about going. I might have stayed. But I knew then she didn't really care about me any more. She had Vince and his son – her new family. I was nothing.

She did call Gary's house. I knew just from her side of the conversation there was still no word about him.

"His poor mum's worried sick," she said, as she put the receiver back.

I was worried too, but I couldn't show it, could I? I shrugged my shoulders. "He'll be fine. Gary's the type that'll always be fine."

Again, it was the wrong thing to say. She couldn't hide the disappointment in her eyes. She picked up her coat. "I'm away to work. Remember, I'm working a double shift tonight."

I stepped in her way. "Don't you ever get fed up supporting him? You work. He doesn't. You're a mug, Mum."

She shrugged my hand away. And were those tears in her eyes? "Vince is my husband, Logan. He's a good man. Why can't you see things the way they really are, Logan? Why is it so hard for you to accept the truth?"

"By what your 'good man' told me last night you won't have to put up with me much longer, eh? We're getting a psychiatrist to talk to the nutter in the family."

"Vince shouldn't have told you that." Her cheeks burned bright red. "I wanted to speak to you about it." She sighed. "And it isn't a psychia—" She couldn't bear to speak the word. "It's just someone for you to talk to. A counsellor. You're scared of something, Logan. There's something wrong with you, and you won't talk to me. You need help."

She moved toward me, as if she was going to hug me. I stepped back, wrapped my arms around myself. Body language: stay well back. Didn't want her near me.

She let out a sigh, and shook her head, finished with me. "I'm trying to do my best for you, Logan. I think you need someone professional to help you."

If I hadn't already made my decision to leave I would have made it then.

"I'll see you tomorrow," she said as she left. "We can talk about it then."

I stood at the window and watched her run across the concourse, heading for the bus stop and the bus that would take her to work, pulling her coat around her against the stiff breeze.

"No, you won't, Mum," I whispered. "You won't see me again."

FORTY-FOUR

I didn't walk to school with Lucie, and I didn't wait for her after school. I tried to avoid her the whole day. I was afraid that if I talked to Lucie I might change my mind about going, and I didn't want to change my mind. I headed home and packed up my rucksack with some food that wouldn't be missed and some fresh clothes and my sleeping bag. Vince had bought it for me, hoping we could go on camping trips together, so we could 'bond'. The sleeping bag had never been used.

Vince wasn't in. So I made myself something to eat and left my dirty dishes in the sink. When he did come in he would assume I had gone out after my tea to meet Baz. Let's face it, he was the only mate I had left.

Baz was waiting for me at the precinct, sitting on the wall outside the takeaway. He had a rucksack swung round his shoulder, and his hoodie was pulled up over his cap. He turned when he saw me and for a second I saw him exactly the way the CCTV camera might have captured him.

"Ready?" he beamed his big white smile at me.

I threw my rucksack in the air. "For anything," I said.

"So how are we travelling?" he asked.

"Pity we can't drive," I said. "We could steal a car."

"Hey, how about if we nick a couple of bikes?" The idea made him laugh. I thought he was serious. He laughed even harder when he saw my reaction. "Hey, don't get skidmarks on your boxers. I'm kidding." He slapped me on the back. "Let's go." He called back to me as he walked. "So, how are we getting to this Aberdeen?"

I suggested we avoid buses and trains for the first couple of days at least.

"So, no bikes, no buses, no trains. Tell me again why we're walking to Aberdeen?" he said.

"Baz, there are CCTV cameras everywhere. I want us to be careful. We'll be spotted. This is the Big Brother age."

"Rubbish. Look at Gary. Now you see him." He snapped his fingers in the air. "Now you don't. Vanished without a trace."

"Maybe there's a reason for that." I said.

"You think they've got him? You think he's wearing a cement overcoat by now?"

I didn't answer that. He was putting into words the terrifying things I'd been thinking.

"No." He shrugged the idea away. "Think about it, illegal immigrants go missing all the time, and escaped convicts, and children. Never found. Don't tell me about Big Brother. If you don't want found in this country..." He swung round, like a magician doing a trick. "You can become invisible."

And do you know, for a moment I half expected him to disappear before my eyes.

"I'd still feel better if we steered clear of the CCTV cameras. I'm not as confident as you are."

"Well, ok, even Confident Baz will go with your wishes. Let's hitch a lift. We'll head for the motorway. The lorry drivers are great, they would stop for us. We could be halfway there before anybody even knows we're gone."

I didn't say anything, but I didn't like the idea of hitching a lift, travelling in the dark with a stranger. My mum's warnings still rang in my ears.

"Come on, what do you think?" he said.

And of course, I gave in to him. "You're the boss."

I let Baz lead us then. He knew this estate. I didn't. We headed through streets and alleys, behind shops. It seemed to take us ages. It was even more exciting because I didn't know where we were going. For all I knew we could have been going round in circles. In fact there were times I was sure we were.

"Haven't we passed this building before?" I pointed to a red car parked outside a block of flats. "I'm sure I've seen that car..."

"Hey, all these tower blocks look alike, and how many red cars are there? I am trying to make sure we're not being followed."

"So you think we are being followed too?"

"You're one paranoid boy, do you know that?"

"Just because you're paranoid doesn't mean they're not after you." It was an old joke but it made Baz laugh and laugh, and after a while I laughed too.

FORTY-FIVE

Yet, as dusk began to fall, I couldn't get over the feeling that we *were* being followed.

"It's all in your imagination," Baz kept telling me when I'd stop and look behind me. "There's no one after us. I told you, the way I'm going, no one could follow us."

I wanted to believe that, so I stopped checking behind us all the time.

"Hey, I've been thinking," Baz said. Then he laughed. "Not something I do often, eh? Who says we find somewhere to kip for the night, and then, first light we head for the motorway?"

I was so relieved. I'd been dreading going on to the motorway, especially at night. "Sounds good to me," I said.

We bought fish and chips from a van on the street. Well, actually I bought it: a big fish supper that we shared between us.

"Have you not got any money?" I asked Baz. He always seemed to hang back when it came to paying.

"Keeping it for when we hit the road. I mean really hit the road. Hey, we're in this together."

He gave me a high five. I gave him one back even though I hate high fives, think they're so phoney. I noticed people looking at us as if we were daft.

We squeezed our way through a broken steel fence into an old junk yard and sat in a corner behind some empty portacabins, eating our fish and chips and talking about what we were going to do next.

"This is the best thing for us, mate," Baz said. "We'll be safe in Aberdeen. Hide out in the Highlands. They'll never find us." He put on a really phoney Scots accent. "We'll rrroam the heatherrr hills," he said, rolling his 'r's. "We'll searrrch oot the Loch Ness monsterrrr."

"Yeah," I agreed. "If they can't find a big thing like Nessie, why should they find us?"

Yet even in the few hours we'd been gone, I had almost forgotten who 'they' were. Distance, time, even a little of it, had made it seem simply like a nightmare. I would wake up soon.

Baz stopped eating. He looked at me as if he was reading my mind. "You don't want to go back do you?"

"No way," I said without hesitation. I didn't want

to go back. What was I going back to? I looked at my watch. Almost 11 o'clock. I still wouldn't be missed. If Vince was home, he would just assume I was out with Baz. He might be annoyed I wasn't in by now, but he wouldn't do anything. I could almost see him, standing by the window, checking his watch. Perhaps going out onto the walkway as if watching for me would bring me home earlier. And Mum's shift didn't finish till well after midnight. She'd remember our argument, and think I was staying out late to annoy her. I'd done that before. She would think I was out with Baz too. It would be tomorrow before either of them realised I wasn't coming back at all. If anyone cared.

And when they did? Who would they call?

Not Claude's mum, or Gary's. Would they be as reluctant as Gary's family to involve the police? But Gary had run away before. I hadn't.

Or had I?

I seemed to have a vague memory that I had, once upon a time. A faint memory from long ago. When I was really young.

Or was that a dream I had once had?

Lucie might miss me. Tomorrow, she might wonder why I hadn't come to school. I pictured her waiting at the park. Checking the time, sitting on a swing, watching for me.

But Lucie wouldn't do anything. She thought I was weird. Hadn't she told me that? "You're as weird as I am," she had once said. "That's why we get on so well." And if she heard that Mum had been planning for 'someone' to talk to me, she'd understand. She'd believe that I would run away rather than that. She was the only one I had told about the fire and my suspicions about the Machans, but she'd say nothing about that.

Would my mum phone Baz? No. My mum didn't have his mobile number, and didn't know his home number either. So it might be another day before they realised we had gone off together.

"Will your Auntie Dorothy miss you?" I asked Baz.

"She always says I'm a big boy, I can take care of myself. Let's me do what I want." He shrugged his shoulders. "I think she might miss me though."

"You're lucky, Baz. They care about you. There's no real reason why you should run. Maybe you should go back. Confess everything. Go to the cops."

It was the thing that sent him spare. He turned on me. "No way! And where you go, mate. I go."

FORTY-SIX

Where you go, I go. Baz would not desert me. It made me feel good when he said that.

Baz stood up. "We have to find somewhere to sleep." He looked around. "Wonder if we can get into any of these portacabins?" He walked around pushing one door after another. Finally he found one that scraped open. He turned to me and smiled. "Your room is ready, sir."

He stepped inside. I followed him. "I'm afraid I'll have to complain about the housekeeping in this hotel." I drew my finger across the windowsill. It was covered in dust. "I'll be on to TripAdvisor about this."

Baz gave a little bow. "I'll have the maid in to clean it

right away. Now would that be continental breakfast in the morning, or the full English, sir?"

We pushed the door closed and Baz laughed as I shoved a brick against it. "I'm taking no chances," I told him. "There's a lot of funny people out there."

It was a gloomy place, but at least it was out of the night cold. Even in summer, nights are chilly in Scotland. I pulled my sleeping bag from my rucksack and spread it on the ground. Baz did the same with his.

He lay on his back, his hands linked under his head. "Just think. No school tomorrow. No alarms. Not for us. Ever again. This is an adventure."

I too wanted to think of it as an adventure. I wanted to stop being afraid. I wished so much I could be fearless like Baz. I tried to sleep, but I couldn't stop thinking about Gary. Had he run away, just as we were running away? Or had someone got to him, just as they had got to Claude? I hated to think of him lying somewhere, legs broken, alone, afraid. At least I wasn't alone. I had Baz.

"I wonder how Claude's doing," I said softly.

"He'll be fine," Baz said. He yawned. "Let's get some shut-eye."

"He looked so scared that night at the hospital, Baz. I wish you'd seen him."

"Yeah, but come on, do you really believe gangsters would say that to him? 'Take your medicine like a man, little boy, and pass on a message to your friends: *Nobody messes with us. We're coming for the lot of you.*' I think he made that up. Heard it in a movie somewhere."

Maybe he did, I thought, as I drifted off to sleep. It was a bit too dramatic.

I woke up at some time during the night. Baz was snoring gently beside me. The brick was still against the door. I looked at my watch. 3.33 in the morning. Had my mother noticed I hadn't come in? I checked my phone. I had three missed calls from her. And three texts.

> Give me a call when you get this.

> Where are you, Logan?!

> Logan, ring me!!

Was she upset? Worried? In tears when she had sent those texts?

I thought of Gary's mum, her eyes red-rimmed from her crying.

And Claude's mum that night at the hospital, weeping and angry.

And Claude too, looking so scared.

And then another thought came to me.

Baz hadn't come to the hospital. He hadn't seen or spoken to Claude. I remember how he cut me off when I tried to tell him what had happened there – what Claude had told us.

So how did he know so exactly what Claude had said that night?

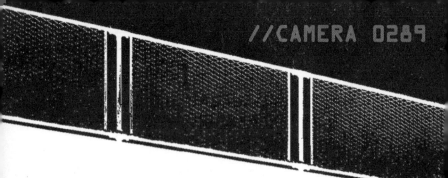

FORTY-SEVEN

Dogs barking woke me just an hour later. I jumped to my feet and nudged Baz with my foot. "Get up!"

He was upright in a flash. We both looked out the small dusty window of the portacabin. A man was heading our way. He had two Rottweilers on a leash, both straining to get away from him.

"Security guy," Baz whispered. "We better hit the road."

"They'll get us. We can't run fast enough." The dogs had begun to growl now, as if they could smell us, smell how close we were.

"He'll not come after us," Baz said. "We're only boys. This is a junkyard, we're not doing anything bad." He nudged me in the ribs, and he winked. "Slip him a couple of quid and he'll forget about us."

He grinned at me, and I tried to grin back, but I thought I remembered a sign. Had it been on the fence outside here?

TRESPASSERS WILL *ALWAYS* BE PROSECUTED

Or eaten by dogs more like, by the sound of those Rottweilers.

Baz grabbed me. "Come on." We rolled up our sleeping bags quickly, stuffed them into our rucksacks. Then Baz was out of the door in a blur of movement. I tried to keep up with him, but I could never run as fast as Baz. I was just steps outside the hut and Baz was already out of sight.

"Hold it!" The man shouted at me. The dogs were going crazy again, barking like mad. I thought for a moment about running on, but then I imagined him unclipping the leash and those dogs running free. I could not outrun them. I froze.

"Hold it!" he said again, as if I wasn't even now standing still. He was a big man with a shaved head. The grey hairs on his chest were trying to escape from the collar of his shirt, and the sleeves were rolled up past his elbows to show his bulging biceps. As he came closer I could see those grey hairs popping out of his nostrils too. His face was heavy and hard. Everybody's idea of a bouncer. "What are you doing here, boy?"

He struggled to hold the Rottweilers back as he walked towards me. I couldn't keep my eyes off those dogs.

"I said, *What are you doing here?*" he asked again.

My mouth was dry. "Me and my mate, we're taking a shortcut home. Sorry, didn't mean any harm."

He looked around. "So where's your mate?"

Baz was gone. Maybe just as well. "He ran on."

"Some mate, eh? Deserting you." He pushed the door of the portacabin open with his torch. Glanced inside. "You smoking in there?"

The barking of the dogs was giving me a headache. I could hardly hear what he was saying. If only they would stop. "Don't smoke. Sorry." Why was I apologising?

"Drinking then?" He took a step toward me, sniffed.

"Honest. No."

Then his face seemed to soften, taking me by surprise. He even managed a hint of a smile. "On your bike, then. But I better not see you here again."

Would he have let me go if Baz had been still with me? Would Baz have been aggressive, challenging him, making fun of the muscles and the hairy nostrils and the shaved head? 'Is this the best job you could get, pal? Security guard in a junk yard. You're not even the B-team, mate.' I could imagine Baz saying that.

He would have made things worse. Yes, bet he would have.

I was off and running the second the man said I could go, hoping he wasn't going to let those Rottweilers off the lead, then stand there laughing as they chased me. I darted behind the other portacabins and the bags of rubbish piled against the walls, I leapt the gate out of the yard, and almost fell on top of Baz.

He caught me, steadied me. He was laughing. "You should see yourself running. Funniest thing I've ever seen."

"I notice you didn't wait for me."

He only shrugged. "No point both of us getting eaten." Then he ran on. "Come on, I'm hungry. Let's get some breakfast."

Of course I paid again. I bought rolls and a carton of milk from a stand in the street. When I found Baz he was sitting on a wall beside a park. He was on his phone.

"Who are you phoning?" I asked him.

He shook his head. "Just checking my messages. Me old auntie called." He laughed, and put on a perfect old lady accent. "Come on, home, my darlin' boy. I'm missing you already."

Goodness, he was good at mimicking voices. "You should be an actor, Baz. I could have sworn that *was* your auntie."

"Multi-talented, that's me."

"So, where are we going?" I asked.

"I still think we should head for the motorway," Baz said. "We can hitch a lift from there."

Would a lorry driver even pick us up?

I wanted to ask him that, but Baz seemed to know what he was doing, and he answered my unasked question. "Lorry drivers are brilliant, always picking up hitchhikers, and they won't tell on us. We'll say we're heading north to spend the weekend with our dads. Give them a sob story about a broken family. And anyway, your mum won't have contacted the cops yet, I bet."

He was right. I had a feeling she would give it a bit more time before she did, hoping she would hear my key in the lock, and the door opening and me stepping in. Plenty of time for us to get a lift and be halfway to Aberdeen.

FORTY-EIGHT

There was hardly anyone around as we trudged through the streets. It was too early. Yet I still couldn't get rid of the feeling that we were being watched. But not one of the few people we passed even looked our way. Men and women heading for work on a sunny summer morning. If our photos ever appeared on television, would they even remember they had seen us as they pushed past? Bet they wouldn't.

I stopped dead when I saw a headline in a news stand as we passed it. It made my blood run cold.

BODY FOUND IN LOCAL DUMP

Baz saw it too. "It's not Gary," he said. "It can't be."

But I had to be sure. I started to go inside the shop. Newsagents are always open from the crack of dawn. Baz held me back. "You buy that paper, and somebody might remember your face. It's not worth the risk. It's not him."

He didn't want it to be Gary either. But for once, I was determined to go against Baz. He waited outside while I bought the paper. He was right of course. The body that had been found was a woman, the victim of some kind of domestic assault. Baz leaned over my shoulder to read it with me. Relief flooded through me. It wasn't Gary.

I pulled out my phone. **Low battery** it proclaimed on the screen. There had been another few missed calls from my mum. I was tempted to call her back. Baz stopped me. "What's the point?" he said. "Unless you're going back. Are you?"

"Of course not," I said quickly.

"Call when you get up to Aberdeen. Call her then."

He checked his watch. "Come on, we're wasting time. Let's go. Aberdeen here we come!"

Aberdeen. You don't know how great that sounded to me. I was tired already, tired of looking over my shoulder, thinking I was being followed. It seemed like a dream, going to Aberdeen. Going back home. I would be safe up north.

"You have got money, haven't you?" I asked Baz again.

"Yeah, yeah, I got money." He held out some notes. "What's wrong with you? Get out of bed the wrong side this morning?" Then he laughed, and usually I couldn't resist laughing back with him. But not this time. "Get the joke?" he said. "We weren't in a bed, eh? Ok." He slipped from the wall. "What's wrong with your face?"

"You only deserted me this morning," I said, though that wasn't what was bothering me.

"Oh come on," Baz said. "If you'd got out of there first you would have kept running too. I would have expected it. And I'm bigger than you, haven't got your sweet, wee innocent face. He wouldn't have let me go so easy."

That was probably true, but that wasn't what I was thinking about. I was remembering my thought when I woke up at 3.33 a.m. "How did you know what Claude said at the hospital?"

He looked totally baffled. "Eh?"

"Last night. You could tell me what Claude said at the hospital, word for word. How did you know? I didn't tell you."

"Yes, you did," he said.

"No. I didn't. I tried to, and you wouldn't let me."

"You must have. Or Gary did. How else would I know?"

And I didn't want to think about how else he could know. It was too scary.

"You're not thinking straight, Logan. Let's get out of here."

He was right about that. I felt as if my head was buzzing. Buzzing with all sorts of strange notions. The calls from Mum, the way we seemed to be stumbling about going nowhere, the strange feeling I had about Baz. Yet when he began to run, I followed him.

As I hurried after him, my phone rang. I looked at the number. Mum again. I ignored it. A moment later a message came up on the screen:

> You have
> 1 voicemail

I wasn't going to listen to it. But couldn't stop myself. I heard my mum's heartbroken voice.

"Where are you? I know you were angry when I saw you last, upset because I said I wanted you to talk to someone. Forget that, you don't have to, you don't have to do anything, but please, Logan, come home. Please. I'm begging you."

She was crying all the way through the message.

Baz looked back at me. "Your mum? Is she upset?"

I nodded. Baz smiled. "This'll teach her a lesson, eh?" The smile didn't stretch to his eyes. He sounded so cold.

Mum's voice was like a knife through my heart. I could picture her clutching the phone, knuckles white, waiting, hoping for it to ring. For me to call her back.

"You're not thinking of calling her are you?" Baz snapped.

I shook my head.

The battery would be dead soon. She wouldn't be able to phone again, and I wouldn't be able to call her. Was that what I wanted? Baz was striding on ahead of me. I shoved the phone back in my pocket and caught up with him.

"Where are we?" We seemed to be heading through some kind of derelict industrial estate.

"Shortcut to the motorway," he said.

"Are you sure you know where you're going?"

He stopped in his tracks and turned back to me, a scowl on his face. "What's that supposed to mean?"

I didn't want to argue with him. I couldn't risk losing Baz. I shrugged. "No offence. We just seem to have been walking for ages, and not getting anywhere."

"This takes us further up on the motorway. We cut off and we're on the road north. I know a spot where the lorries park. We need somewhere lorries can stop and pick us up, don't we?"

I hadn't thought of that. I apologised right away. "Sorry, Baz. On you go."

My phone buzzed again. Baz heard it too. He turned to me. "Don't answer it."

I held back. Let it ring till it stopped. And Baz grinned. I'd done what he wanted, again. Why did I do that? A moment later there was a ping on the phone. It was a text. I stopped again, took the phone from my pocket.

> Logan, come home. I love you so much. Please come home.

I could imagine Mum's fingers trembling as she typed that in. Bet she had to type it more than once. She always made mistakes when she would text; Vince and I would laugh at her autocorrect fails and some of the crazy messages she sent. But this text was perfect.

I love you so much.

I could hear her sobs as she typed that in, see the tears running down her face. My mum loved me. I'd always known she loved me. Why was I doing this? Why was I hurting her so much? Why was I running away from the one person I could trust? The one person who would help me?

"Come on," Baz said. As if he expected me to follow.

Why was I following Baz? Why did I always follow Baz? There was a part of me beginning not to trust him.

The text message pinged again, urging me to answer.

> I love you so much, Logan.

"Trying to get round you, eh?"

I couldn't look at Baz. I was biting my lips so hard, you know the way you do when you are trying to stop yourself from crying? But I couldn't let Baz see me cry, could I?

"You want to go back, don't you?"

And I knew in the moment when Baz said it, my decision had been made.

I looked at him, and nodded. What was I doing all this for? All this running away. What was I really running away from?

"If these people are as bad as we think, they'll come after us. Aberdeen won't be far enough. And if they can't find us... maybe they'll turn on my mum." I couldn't bear the thought of anyone hurting her.

"And what are you going to do when you go back?"

"Tell my mum everything." I wished I had done that before. "About the fire, about the Machans. Everything. I'm not going to run any more."

I knew it was the right thing as soon as I said it.

"I thought you were worried she would put you into care?"

I shrugged. "She won't do it unless she has to." And

maybe, after all, it would be the best for me. Something *was* wrong with me. I was beginning to realise that.

For the first time I felt I was thinking clearly. This was the right thing to do.

"And the polis? You gonny tell them everything as well?"

I nodded, waiting for him to explode. "Are you with me?"

That big smile spread across his face. "I told you before, where you go, I go."

I was going home. I didn't care what happened. I wanted to be free of this fear. I wanted my mum. Baz walked on ahead of me, he took out his phone. Walked away from me, turning his back.

"Who are you calling?" I asked him.

"My old auntie. Just texting her to tell her I'm on my way. Just in case she does anything crazy."

Maybe I should call my mum, I thought. I pulled out my phone again, and pressed our number on speed dial. The screen went black, that little circle began spinning so fast I felt dizzy. I was out of battery.

Didn't matter. I was going home.

FORTY-NINE

We were only a few blocks from my flats when I saw them. Two men sitting in a car. The car was moving very slowly, as if it had been cruising about the streets. They were looking for someone... Looking for *me*. I stood still. I couldn't move. Their eyes swept the street from one side to the other. And before I could make my legs work, they had caught sight of me. The car ground to a halt. The two men were out in an instant.

They were dressed in suits, they could have passed as businessmen, but there was a hard look on each of their faces. They didn't run, not at first. They began striding straight towards us.

I still couldn't get my legs to move. "B–Baz." My voice

233

was a trembling whisper. He was still walking on. Why hadn't he seen them? "Baz!" My voice was more strident this time.

Baz stopped, and turned quickly. When he saw my face he glanced back and I knew he had clocked them at last. "Follow me," he mouthed, and nodded to the road beside us.

The men's stride became a run, and that's when we both bolted. I had never run so fast. My feet pounded on the pavements so hard my soles ached. Baz was well in front of me and I prayed I wouldn't lose him. I didn't want to be alone, not with those men behind me.

We ran over gardens, up back closes, leaping over fences, and then up streets again. There was still hardly anyone about. I barely dared look to see if they were still behind us. But I could hear them. It was Baz who stopped and turned. He looked beyond me. "I don't see them. Maybe we've lost them."

"How did they find us, Baz?"

He shrugged. "They've been watching your house. Waiting for you." He looked around again. No sign of them. "Come on, we'll try to make it back to your place."

I took one step and stopped again. "No." I said. "I'm not leading them back to my mum."

"Well, where are we going to go then?"

I didn't have an answer to that. Go into a shop? Just

ask for help? But what if the shopkeeper was paying protection money to the Machans?

Baz pulled me on. "Come on, we can't stop now."

So I ran on behind him. Hoping against all hope we could outrun them.

FIFTY

I felt my whole body shaking as I ran. They had found us. Last on their list. Me and Baz. 'Take your medicine like a man,' they had said to Claude. Now they were ready to dish it out to us.

Baz darted into a doorway, I ran in with him. He was as breathless as I was.

"I can't believe they're still after us." I said. "We're only boys. What do they want from us?"

"Teaching us a lesson," he said breathlessly. "We were at the fire. We got Mad Mike arrested." He kicked at the wall angrily. "And we stole those Xbox games too."

"We?" It wasn't fair. It was Baz who had stolen the

games, not me. He had pushed the games to me and I had pushed them back, how could he not remember that? Yet, even then, I couldn't bring myself to say it to him. Because after all… what had those surveillance cameras shown? Me, with the games in my hands. And it was Baz who had dared Al Butler to start the fire, not me. But what was the point of saying that now?

Baz went on. "No one messes with the Machans."

"What will they do to us if they catch us, Baz?"

He didn't answer. And I saw, for the first time, real fear in his face. We had both heard the horror stories of what they could do, these people. They were ruthless, capable of anything. Even to boys like us. What had they done to Gary?

I heard running feet, heading down the empty street. Still after us. We moved back, pressed ourselves further into the doorway. I think we both wished we could melt into the steel panels of the door. I had never seen Baz look scared. He was always cocky, sure of himself, now he looked really frightened. Beads of sweat dripped down his face.

Or maybe that wasn't fear I saw at all. Did he look guilty too? And why should I think that?

How had they found us? It was as if they had known we were heading home, had been waiting for us.

And I remembered that phone call. He had walked away, turned his back on me, said he'd texted his auntie.

But is that what he had really been doing? I pushed the thought away. I was being paranoid. I had to trust Baz. He was all I had left.

The sound of running feet faded into the distance. It had only been an early morning worker hurrying for his bus.

"Let's go." Baz pulled at me, and, again, I followed.

We turned a corner, and we were in a part of the estate that looked familiar. It was open ground. Here a lot of the houses had been demolished to make way for new builds, the streets were eerily empty, with weeds covering the road and the pavements. I almost panicked. There was nowhere to hide. We ran on and I saw with relief a long line of lock-up garages and empty flats, boarded up ready to be demolished.

"Down here," Baz waved; we turned a corner into an alley of lock-ups – then panic did set in. I knew where we were. I recognised the alley we had run into.

"This is a dead end!" I tried not to shout.

The dead end we had led the Young Bow into. They had followed us here, and we had trapped them, and now we were in the same trap.

"What did you bring us here for?" Baz was supposed to know where he was going. "It's a dead end!"

He was shaking his head. Still refusing to admit he could ever be wrong. He was looking all around. "No! Look!" He pointed to the big warehouse with the signs on its windows and walls.

TO BUY OR **LEASE**

It was locked tight shut, no help to us. Except... except for a one small broken panel in a window. Men couldn't get through there. But boys could.

Baz saw it too. "Let's get in here," he said. "This is a good place. Come on."

We took another look round. A car passed at the end of the alley, but there was no one about. I imagined those men running after us, crossing the open waste ground, seeing the lock-ups and the flats. They would soon be checking one alley after another. We couldn't outrun them, but maybe we could hide from them.

"They're going to get to the end of that alley, they might even run up here, but they'll see it's a dead end, no sign of us, and they'll think we've run on somewhere else. Right?" Baz said.

"Yeah, right," I was still afraid, but I could see the sense in that. There was no time to waste, and I pulled over a couple of crates that were lying around, and laid one on top of the other beneath the broken window. I climbed up. The jagged opening was small. I turned to

Baz. "I can just make it through," I said to him. "Will you?"

Baz nodded. "I can make it if you can."

I gripped the window to pull myself up and the broken glass cut into my hands. Blood bubbled on my palm, but I felt no pain. I just wanted to get inside. I smashed the glass even more, made a wider opening for Baz, then I pushed myself through.

I jumped to the floor, looked around. It was a big empty warehouse, built on two floors. There were a couple of rooms at the back, offices maybe, and a steel staircase rising to the upper floor. We could hide here, till it was safe to move on.

Move on where? a voice inside my head asked.

One thing at a time, I can't think further than this moment.

FIFTY-ONE

Baz was right, those men wouldn't think we'd be in here. They would come up the alley, see it was a dead end and they would head back down and run on. We'd be safe here, for a while anyway.

"We should call the police," I said. "Now's the time." But I had no battery. My phone was dead.

Baz looked at his phone. "Same," he said.

"What are we gonna do?" I asked.

Baz stepped away from me. "We should hide in two different places. I'll go in the back." He pointed to what looked like one of the offices.

I wanted to go with him. Didn't want us to separate. *Why couldn't we just stay together?* But I couldn't bring myself to say that to him.

I didn't have to say it. Baz obviously knew what I was thinking. "We're better being separate. If one of us gets caught, the other can run, then we can contact the cops." He pushed me away from him. "No time to talk, Logan. You go up the stairs. There's bound to be somewhere up there. Maybe even another window you can get out of, a fire escape or something." He was already backing away from me. "If you get a chance to escape, take it, I'll understand. If anything happens. Just go," he said.

I looked up the rickety steel staircase. Would there be somewhere up there to hide? I held back.

"Go!" Baz said again. "They're not even going to come in here. We'll be safe." He tried a smile, but it didn't work, not this time. "We'll give it half an hour... then we'll come out. Ok?"

And then, I was alone. Baz disappeared into the office and I was left on my own. I looked up. Pigeons had nested among the steel rafters. One of them fluttered in the roof and then was gone. The stairs clanged as I climbed. I stopped and tried to tiptoe, I was making too much noise. Thoughts were whirling in my head: what we should have done, what we shouldn't have done. We should have run on. We shouldn't have come into this dead-end alley. Why had we come into this warehouse? But maybe Baz was right, maybe it was a good place. Those men, they must have run past. If they'd been coming, they would be here by now. I stopped halfway up, listening for the sound of their running footsteps outside. Nothing. We could wait here, perhaps till nightfall then... Go to the first police station we could find. That was what I decided to do. Easier to decide that without Baz arguing about it. I began to climb again. I'd find a place up here and wait. Give myself time to think. I needed time to think.

There was no office up here. No window either. No handy fire escape. Nothing except rows of steel shelving stacked up right at the back against the wall. I could hide in behind them. I stepped warily over some heavy plastic pipes lying on the floor, covered in dust.

I walked to the very back wall, then crouched down and began pushing my rucksack ahead of me. I crawled behind the last row of the steel shelving then I huddled in the corner, hugging my knees. I hadn't prayed in a long time, but I prayed now. They wouldn't come. I kept telling myself that. They hadn't seen us climbing in here. They would have run past the alley, were probably still running.

Please.

My foot knocked against something on the floor. It was a screwdriver with a red handle, left by some workman. I picked it up. Would I have the nerve to use it as a weapon if I had to? I held it tight in my palm and winced with pain.

My hand dripped blood. I remembered with horror the way I had cut it as I squeezed through the window.

Saw again my blood dripping down the jagged glass. My blood would still be there on the glass, on the sill. Fresh blood. If they looked they would see it. They would know we had come through that window, and into this warehouse.

My teeth chattered with fear.

But if they didn't come up this alley they wouldn't even see the blood. And even if they did, they could never get through that broken window the way Baz and I had done. The thought comforted me for a moment.

But they didn't need to come through the window, did they?

They had the keys to front door.

FIFTY-TWO

I didn't hear the door opening. I only saw the light stream in as it swung wide. I waited. I listened. I bit into my hand to stop my teeth chattering. I could feel cold sweat dripping down my face. I heard footsteps and, though they must have only been whispering, the echoes of their quiet voices carried up to the rafters. As if those pigeons had caught the words in their beaks and had flown up here with them. Were they the same men who had been after us? I knew they must be. Those whispers had a menacing quality. Had Baz heard them too? Maybe if there was a window in that office downstairs he might already be gone. I wouldn't blame him. I could imagine his long legs stretching as he went through another window. He could run for the police. He would run for the police.

No window for me. The only chance I had was to stay here, quiet as death, still as a corpse. Maybe they'd give up, go away. Look for us somewhere else.

Did these people ever give up?

There was no sound. My breathing was all I could hear and it was too loud. I tried to stop breathing. I really did. I was terrified to move. I listened and held tight to the screwdriver.

Nothing. I hoped for a moment that they had gone.

Maybe it was a trap. Maybe they were waiting for me. I imagined them on the stairs, ready to spring at me if I emerged from this hiding place.

I was desperate to scratch my nose. How stupid was that? And I didn't dare. The tiniest movement would make too much noise. That scratch would be like steel claws being dragged down a blackboard.

Then I heard the sound of feet on steel. One of them was climbing up that stairway, heading to where I was. Clang, clang, clang. Moving steadily. Not in any hurry. As if they already knew I was trapped.

But they still might not find me. Not know I was there. Not if I was quiet enough. They couldn't possibly see me here. I tried to fold myself behind the steel, merge into the metal.

Had they already got Baz? Was he even now being held by the other man, downstairs, a hand clamped over his mouth? My whole body was shaking with fear. Was

Baz shaking too? Bet he wasn't. No, not Baz. He'd still be full of that bravado of his. He'd be spitting at them, struggling against them. Trying to bite into the man's hand. How I wished I had some of that bravado now.

I had none of his boldness. I was just me. Useless me. And I knew then, no matter what I did, they were going to get me.

This was karma.

That was what the Asian man on the television had called it. Karma. You repay for all you do, good or bad.

What goes around, comes around.

The man had reached the top of the stairs now and I watched his feet approaching under the row of shelving. He couldn't see me, but he would any minute. He would crouch down and peer under and there would be a look of triumph on his face. Gotya! The feet stepped closer. All I could see were shiny brown leather shoes.

I couldn't stay still any longer. Attack is the best form of defence. I'd read that somewhere. This was the only chance I would have. If I waited any longer I would be in his clutches, too late to do anything. I sprang to my feet, and pushed hard at the steel shelving. It began to topple and fall with a crash and a clatter. I saw his feet step back hurriedly, but he couldn't avoid them completely. He let out a yell as the steel fell against his legs, trapping him. I didn't give him a second to think. I jumped past him. A stubby tanned hand shot out from beneath the steel and tried to grab me. He caught at my ankle and

I stumbled and rolled on the floor away from him, but he still reached out to me. I stabbed at his hands with the screwdriver. It caught him and he drew it back with a yell of pain. He was still trapped under the steel. I shot to my feet again. Then suddenly I realised there were two of them up here. The other one had come up the stairs too when he heard his partner yell. Relief flooded through me. Yes, relief. Because if the two of them were up here... then there was no one down there. If I made it to the ground, I could be out of here and off. Safe.

The other man was at the top of the stairs, barring my way. He was built like a sumo wrestler, bursting out of the suit he was wearing. I was quick. I was young. Maybe even smarter than them. I rolled a long plastic pipe that was lying on the floor at him. Then another and another. He had to jump to dodge them, but stumbled and fell back, away from the stairs. I didn't waste any time. I ran. If I could make it down, I could get out. I could get out again through that window, or even through the door if they'd left it open. I think I almost leapt the whole flight. Glanced back for an instant to see how close he was behind me. And he wasn't close enough. Still at the top of the stairs. Not even rushing to come down.

I was going to make it.

In that same second another hand grabbed me and I was hauled back with such force I was sent sprawling along the floor. "Going somewhere, son?"

There were three of them.

FIFTY-THREE

I'd been tricked. Two of them had come after me. I just hadn't considered that there might be a third down here. He was a big man, a flick of brown hair over his forehead, a long face and great fat cheeks. He looked like a horse – that was my thought at that moment. Then I had a sudden cold feeling. I had seen him somewhere before. I swayed when I realised who he was.

This was Mad Mike Machan himself.

He just stood there, watching me, and smiling. I couldn't see any way out of this now. I sat up, dragged myself back so I had my back against the wall.

And that was when I saw Baz.

He was stepping softly behind Machan. I tried not to

look at him. Maybe Machan didn't know Baz was there. Maybe Baz had an escape plan. He'd get out, get the police.

He looked up at me. He looked nervous. Could I blame him for that? No.

I dared a glance and saw him run his tongue along his lips.

"Can I go now?" His voice echoed in that tin coffin of a building. "I told you where he was. Can I go now?"

Now I looked straight at him. I stared at him. I'm sure my jaw dropped. What was he saying? What did he mean?

Machan followed my eyes. Baz began to back away from him. "You said you wouldn't do anything to me if I told you where he was. You promised."

Baz was leaving. Leaving me alone.

"Baz!" I shouted after him.

Machan turned back to me. His smile was a slash of menace. "No one's going to help you now, son," he said.

And when I looked back, Baz was no longer there. I could still hear him, hear his footsteps pounding away. He was hauling open the door, knew he could get out that way. He hadn't even looked back.

Baz was gone.

FIFTY-FOUR

He'd betrayed me. Baz had betrayed me. Someone I had trusted so much had betrayed me? Had he led me here, knowing they would come? I remembered that phone call I had seen him making – no text message to Auntie Dorothy. Of course not. How did he know how to contact them? How long had it been going on? Was he the black figure who had attacked Claude? Wasn't that what I had feared? Was that how he had known exactly what Claude had said? Because he was there? And had he been the one who poisoned Mickey's dog? Had it all started then? Had he contacted them, told them he knew how to get us all, as long as they let him be? Brave bold Baz, the boy I had admired so much, had been the most cowardly of us all.

In those first seconds it was all I could think about. He had raced out of this warehouse, leaving me alone.

Alone.

It was the clatter of feet on the steel stairs that brought me out of that nightmare, and into another. I swung round. Two men stood on the stairs. The one who had been trapped under the steel was trying to brush himself down. He glared at me and called me a few names I can't repeat here. "You're not making this easy on yourself, son," he finished.

"Take your medicine like a man," the sumo wrestler said. He sounded Welsh, a big broad Welshman – a bull of a man. Was that the same voice Claude had heard? "It'll be over soon."

I tried to stop my voice, my whole body, from shaking. "What are you going to do to me?" I tried to get to my feet. My knees were buckling under me. I gripped the stair rail to stop myself from falling. I didn't wait for their answer. Didn't want it really. "I didn't do anything. I don't know why you're after me. I never done nothing." Why couldn't I stop my voice from whining? I had always wanted to be like Baz – bold, cheeky, unafraid. But Baz had betrayed me. Baz was more of a coward than I was. There was no one I could be like now. He had run out of here, terrified. He had brought them here to get me, so he could be safe.

The men behind me suddenly closed in. Their hands gripped my elbows, lifted me off my feet. "I'm sorry, for whatever you think I've done. I'm sorry." Was I screaming? I hope not. "Let me go."

"'Fraid that's not an option," Machan said. "You boys have caused me no end of problems. Destroying my property, stealing what was mine. Getting the police interested in me. I can't let anybody off with that." He took a step closer. "And *you*, you were the worst of them."

Me? I wanted to shout out to him. *It was Baz, not me!* Had he blamed me for everything? What had Baz told them?

I shook my head, but I couldn't get any words out.

"And that's why I had to come to deal with you for myself. You should be honoured. I don't often do that."

All the time he spoke, I struggled, but they were so strong, used to handling struggling victims.

Victims. The word itself made me feel faint.

I was sweating blood. Images flooded my mind from films I'd seen, documentaries I'd watched, images of what these people were capable of. Noses slashed off, bodies in cement, bullets in the brain, and Claude with his two broken legs.

"You've given me a lot of trouble. But after this, you'll have learned your lesson. You'll never give me any trouble again."

He was enjoying it. He was enjoying seeing my fear, and I so wanted to be brave.

My feet dragged along the floor as the men pulled me into the middle of the warehouse. Machan stepped aside, and what I saw made me yell with terror and struggle even more.

A solitary chair, ropes round the arms and legs to secure me. And the chair was sitting on a big square of plastic sheeting.

Oh dear Lord, what were they going to do to me?

FIFTY-FIVE

That plastic sheeting scared me more than anything else. How I struggled, trying to pull away from them.

Machan only laughed. "Come on, *man up*, son, as they say." Every word was a growl.

I kicked out and caught one of them on the shin, but that only made him angry and I saw he was the one I had stabbed with the screwdriver. The back of his hand still bled. He tightened his hold on me. His fingers bit into my arm. They were pulling, lifting, dragging me toward the chair, I couldn't stop them. They had their orders. They wouldn't go against Mad Mike. They would do whatever they were told to do. They had no feelings about it, one way or another. No pity. Nothing was going to stop them. What they'd done to Al Butler, to Claude, to Gary... Oh dear Lord, what had they done to Gary?

I had another burst of strength, fighting against them, terror made me strong. I heard a bird in the rafters, one of the pigeons. One of the men looked up but only for a second, and then he turned back. My arms were pinioned to the chair, and in seconds I was trussed like a chicken. My arms, and my legs held tight.

Machan was standing behind me. I couldn't see what he was doing. What he was about to do. The others stood before me, their hands clasped in front of them.

Another pigeon flew into the roof. I heard its wings fluttering. Wished I could fly too. Fly off and away.

Let me fly.

"It'll be all over soon, son," Machan said, as he came from behind me, and pulled a knife from his pocket. A Swiss army knife. He swivelled it open and the blades came alive. They fluttered apart with wings of steel.

That made me thrash about all the more, pounding my feet on the ground, shaking the chair. All my struggles only seemed to amuse them.

And Machan took a step closer.

FIFTY-SIX

And right then, right at that moment, the cavalry arrived.

Black uniforms burst into the warehouse, seemed to come from nowhere, rifles at their shoulders, calling out harsh orders:

"Drop the knife!"

"Get away from the boy!"

The blade was dropped on the plastic. One of the men tried to run. A black uniform stopped him with the butt of his rifle. The man fell to the ground.

Someone ran towards me, I could only see his eyes. I couldn't talk. My tongue wouldn't work. I wanted to say, 'Thank you! Thank you! Thank you!' But I couldn't talk.

The policeman untied the ropes. His voice was gentle. "Come on, son. You're safe now."

I tried to stand up. My legs wouldn't work either. They buckled under me. The room swam around me. My rescuer held me up so I wouldn't fall. He called over to another black uniform to help him. Together they just about carried me out of the warehouse. The whole world seemed to be swarming in black. They'd come for me. They'd saved me.

The last thing I saw as I left the warehouse was Machan, hands cuffed behind him, his face dark with anger.

It was only as I sat in the police car, a blanket wrapped round my shoulders that I found my voice. "Where's Baz?"

The PC in the front seat looked round. "Baz?"

It had been a faint hope. That Baz had been responsible for my rescue. That he had run from the warehouse, run to the police, brought them here. Saved me.

Of course it hadn't been Baz. There had been no time. Only minutes had passed from him running away till the police had come crashing in to save me. This had been a well-timed, planned operation. They were too fully prepared with guns and body armour for it not to be.

No, Baz had left me. Betrayed me. I had to face that.

I hated him then. But even hate was overcome by relief. Every other feeling was nothing to that.

I was safe. I had been saved from whatever horror they had in store for me. Nothing else mattered.

FIFTY-SEVEN

They took me to the station, and a doctor came to check me out. All of this passed over me like a dream. People walked past me, they spoke to me, I heard them talk, but I couldn't tell you what they said. I didn't ask about Baz. I'd never ask about him again. He was gone, and I was still stupidly loyal enough to him not to get him involved if the police knew nothing about him.

They told me my mother had been informed I was safe and she would be coming soon. I wondered how she would react, and how much they had told her.

A man came along and sat with me. I think he was some kind of child protection officer. He touched my arm to comfort me, but he said little. Then they took me into a room, and that's where they showed me the CCTV footage. It was night of the fire. The night Al Butler had torched that warehouse. "Do you remember this?"

Of course I did. There was a smoky haze over the fuzzy pictures, almost as if the fire had already been started. And I remembered the eerie red glow of the emergency lighting. And then into plain sight came the guy who had been shot. Al Butler. He turned his face to the camera, just for an instant. His eyes were bright pinpoints of light.

They froze the frame. "Do you recognise him?"

I didn't have to lie. "He was killed, wasn't he?"

"Murdered," the cop said. "Executed."

"Do you know why?" the other cop said.

I didn't say anything.

"Because of this." He jabbed a finger at the screen. "The man who owned this warehouse and most of the properties around it is the gentlemen who was about to use you as a pincushion. A certain Michael Machan."

I nodded.

"Can you see where we're headed here?" the other policeman said.

And still I said nothing. Not because I didn't want to, I just didn't know where to start.

"Let's see some more." He switched the film on again. The dead man, Al Butler, came alive and moved on. Another figure came into view. He turned and it was Mickey. You could hardly make him out; he had a grimace on his face, trying to look scary. But it was Mickey all right. They didn't pause the footage at Mickey. He moved off in a blur and then there was Claude. I could tell without even seeing his face it was Claude. Couldn't mistake that lumbering run of his. The frame froze again.

"You know this boy, don't you?"

I found my voice at last. But it came out like a scratch. "Claude," I said.

"Yes, your friend Claude. Him with the two broken legs. And you know now who was responsible for that?"

The man beside me spoke up. "You can't question him till his mother gets here."

The policeman held up his hand. "I'm not questioning him. I just want him to see this footage. Ok, son?"

The screen moved again. There was me, grinning like an idiot at the camera as if I was so cool, clearly holding those Xbox games. How stupid I looked now. The frame froze again.

"Easy to spot you, Logan."

I only nodded. The screen moved again. And then there was Gary. We'd been laughing at Mickey and Claude and their ghost dance. And there he was, laughing, leaping, punching the air. The frame stopped again leaving him in mid air.

"Wondering what happened to your pal?"

I'd been terrified to mention him. He was dead. I was waiting for them to say it.

But they didn't. The policeman stood up and opened the door.

And Gary walked in.

FIFTY-EIGHT

I jumped from my seat. Gary stepped back quickly as if I would attack him. I wanted to hug him.

"I thought you were..." I didn't finish.

"This is the boy who saved your life," the cop said.

I looked at the policeman and then back to Gary. I didn't understand.

"He came to us. Eventually. Told us everything. We've been after Machan for a long time. And after that fire, though we didn't think Machan was behind it – not his style – we got him in for questioning. But we hadn't a clue you boys were involved in any way. Why should we? We knew Machan must have had the CCTV footage, though he denied it. And if he had it, he'd kept it for a reason. So we began watching him and his enforcers very closely. We knew they were looking for someone, didn't think it might be boys like you."

Gary butted in. "So even when Claude was attacked, they didn't think it had anything to do with the Machans. They really did think it was just another gang."

The policeman continued. "But then your friend came to us, just in time, as it turns out. So we knew you were in a lot of danger. We didn't even know you'd left home; we planned to pick you up today. But we were keeping an eye on the two men who came after you. They were looking for somebody, and suddenly we realised it was you, Logan. When our men saw them run, they ran too. Called it in right away, that's why we were so prepared to rescue you. Machan's men led us to you. But that's all thanks to this boy here." He patted Gary on the back.

I looked at Gary. "You went to the cops."

Gary's top lip was moist with perspiration. He wiped it away. "Not at first. I just ran off. I hid. But after a few days, I knew there was nowhere else to go. I was scared."

"Thank God you did."

I saw the relief flood through him. "I didn't know what else to do." Gary sat down beside me. "They've been great." He nodded at the policeman.

It was the policeman who began to talk. "With that CCTV footage, the Machans managed to identify every one of you. If we'd had it, we could have found you sooner. If you'd come to us right away none of this would have happened."

"How did you get it?" I asked.

"Search warrant for Machan's place."

"Will you be able to make it stick this time?" I remembered that Mad Mike always managed to slip through their fingers.

The policeman smiled. "Yeah, we've got that CCTV footage and a couple of Machan's boys are singing like nightingales about what they've done. And of course, the icing on the cake... Mad Mike caught in the act." He stood up. "You boys must be hungry. How about if I get you something to eat?"

"I could go a sandwich," Gary said.

Me? I couldn't think about food. But I asked for a sandwich too. I just wanted the police out of the room. I wanted to be left alone with Gary. I had so much to tell him. I looked at the other man, this child protection officer. He nodded as if he understood. "I'll let you two boys talk," he said.

As soon as the door closed, Gary leaned toward me and said softly. "I had to tell them we were at that fire. Honest. I was too scared not to."

"I don't care, Gary. You saved me. They had me, that Mad Mike was gonny..." I couldn't bear thinking of what he had intended to do to me. "Thanks Gary."

"We were stupid, Logan... but we didn't deserve all this."

I was so relieved to hear that. "They rescued me, Gary, right in the nick of time. If they hadn't come then..." I felt faint again. Paused before I could carry on. "Anyway, the cops burst in. I honestly cannot remember much about what happened next. I think I was probably in shock. Maybe I still am. And before you ask, Gary..." How I hated saying this. I felt it took me an age to go on, but when I did I just rattled everything out. "Baz left me. I don't know how long he's been working with the Machans. But he has, I'm sure of it. Did it to save himself. I think he poisoned Mickey's dog. Maybe even helped them attack Claude, I don't know. I still hope I'm wrong about that. But he phoned them, told them where I would be, led me to that dead end, to that warehouse, so they could get me. All so they wouldn't hurt him. He's a coward. He deserted me." I swung my hand at the monitor. The screen was still paused at Gary leaping in the air. My voice rose with every word. "And d'ye know what else? He's the only one who managed to avoid being in any of this CCTV footage. The only one. Eh? What about that? Bet he did that on purpose, Gary. I trusted him. We all trusted him. I even went on the run with him. And he left me. Baz betrayed me. He grassed us all up so they wouldn't come after him."

Some stupid loyalty kept me from mentioning Baz to the police, but I wanted Gary to know his treachery.

Gary stared at me. He glanced at the screen, and

then he looked at me. Looked for a long time. Couldn't believe what I was saying, probably.

But then he said the words that changed my life.

"Who's Baz?"

FIFTY-NINE

I thought I'd heard him wrong at first. "Who's Baz? Is that what you just said? Who's Baz?"

He stiffened, nodded. "Yeah, who is this 'Baz'?"

"Baz. We run about with him. Our mate. Your mate. You know who I mean. *Baz*."

"The only other mates I've got are Claude and Mickey." Gary began to stand up. He looked a bit scared. "So, who are you talking about?"

"You're winding me up, Gary." I stood up too. "Baz. You know who Baz is." Gary took a step away from me. There was a look of total disbelief on his face. "It was Baz who got us to go follow Al Butler into that warehouse. It was Baz dared him to torch it. Double dared him, remember? It was Baz, leading us on, manipulating us. I see that now, Gary. We did things to please him, to keep him happy because we were scared of him. Scared to go against him. *Baz!*" I yelled his name. Gary was really beginning to annoy me. What was his game?

"See, there you go again. One minute you seem normal, you're funny, you make us all laugh, we're able to talk to you, and the next second you change, you're like a bleeding Jeckyll and Hyde. *You're* the one who made us go into the warehouse that night. *You* were the one dared Al Butler to set it on fire. The only person I was ever scared of... was *you!*" He yelled out that last word.

I lunged at him. Grabbed him by the collar. "Don't say that!" I hit him with such force we both fell back and landed on the floor. "Don't lie to me. You know Baz. Tell me you know Baz." I began to shake him. "Tell me you know Baz!"

Next minute I was being hauled to my feet. A policeman had run in and had me by the arm. Gary scrambled back from me. "He's off his chump. He's talking about some guy I don't know. Some guy who doesn't exist. Some guy called Baz."

I struggled to get away from the police. "But you know I'm not lying, Gary. Baz does exist. Baz is real."

SIXTY

But Baz wasn't real. He never had been. I learned that over the next few days. Talking to doctors, listening to Gary's statements, and Claude's and Mickey's too. There had never been a Baz. There was only me.

Did that mean I was mad? It was all I wanted to know. Of course, the doctors all told me it didn't. I was just 'disturbed', and 'needed help', and I would get over it, with treatment. They've even got a name for what's wrong with me. Some kind of 'disassociative identity disorder'.

I had to go over everything, again and again, and I still don't understand it.

They said it all began when my dad ran off and left

me and Mum. Yeah, left us. He's not dead. He just walked out one day, and left. I couldn't face up to him leaving, they told me, I missed him so much. Ran away a couple of times trying to find him when he didn't want found. He was no way the dream-dad I had made up. There never were days on the beach with the kites, or football matches together. He never took me anywhere. He didn't care about me, and because I didn't want to believe that, I told myself he was dead. That was when I began to avoid the truth about everything.

My mum was getting really worried about me, between running away and missing school, I was mixing with the wrong people, getting into all sorts of trouble, getting excluded, being picked up by the police. They had suggested taking me into care: I was out of control, they told her. And she couldn't bear that. She fought for me all the way. So when she met Vince, and he suggested we all move to Glasgow to get away from everything in Aberdeen, she agreed.

Mum thought I needed a whole change, things would get better when we were down here. I would be able to come to terms with my dad leaving. I'd be away from all the bad influences up in Aberdeen. But *I* was the real bad influence, and you can't get away from yourself.

I was so afraid when I moved here to Glasgow. I was so alone. No one would like me. If my dad couldn't like me, and if he'd gone off and left me, then how could I expect anyone else to? So they say that was why I created Baz that first day when the boy I'd called a loon was ready to thump me. In that moment I became Baz. No wonder the boy looked so freaked out. In a split second, he saw me changing. Changing from me to Baz. Baz stepped in and saved me, he was the friend who was scared of nothing. So real to me I could see him, talk to him. I had been told I was easily led, and that's why I got into trouble in Aberdeen. So I created someone who wasn't easily led. He was the leader, the one who manipulated other people. Baz was everything I wanted to be.

I wanted to be friends with the boys, but I didn't think they would want me as their friend. So at times, in the blink of an eye, I became Baz. Baz who could be funny. Baz who could be bossy. Baz who could be scary.

But you know, now I see the doctors were right to get me to write this all down, because I can look back and take in all the things I missed at the time.

The boys never referred to Baz by name. Did you notice that? I didn't. They never mentioned his name once. The boys were never scared of Baz. It was me who scared them when I became Baz. My hero. I was the one who wanted to follow Al Butler into that warehouse. I was the one who dared him to drop the match. I was the one who had stolen the Xbox games that night. I was the one who had sold them on the way home, so I was the one with the money.

Baz hadn't been on the CCTV footage because he didn't exist.

And of course he knew what Claude had said at the hospital. Because I knew. I was there.

And when I ran away and thought we were going round in circles, we really were. Because, of course, I didn't know where we were going, did I?

Even when we had gone on the run, hadn't I only bought one fish supper between us? Baz had never come with me to get them, never put his hand in his pocket to buy anything. And when we ran into that dead end, didn't you wonder why Baz didn't leap up onto the roof of the lock-ups and help me up so we could escape over the roof the way we'd done before? We didn't do it, because I could never have got up there by myself. We'd needed Gary's height getting away from the Young Bow.

Baz. Always in the background. My dark secret. He had seemed like flesh and blood to me, but the doctors say he was everything I wanted to be, that's why he felt so real.

But that day we spent in Glasgow, just me and the boys, remember? How relieved I was that Baz wasn't there. That was all me. That's when I began to realise it was better without Baz. That maybe I didn't need him. Baz, or the part of me that was Baz, was making me do things I didn't want to do. Making the other boys do things too. I wanted rid of him, I wanted away from Baz, and the doctors say that was me beginning to get better. Becoming more me, and less Baz. Having Baz betray me was the final sign that I was getting rid of him for good.

I'd got it all wrong with my mum, too. She'd moved here to get me away from all the bad memories I had in Aberdeen. She'd left a house and a job she loved, because things were going so wrong for me up there. She was terrified I would be taken into care if we stayed there any longer. Devastated herself when my dad left, she had no time to grieve about him, because she had only thought of me. My mum, always trying to do the best for me.

And Vince? How wrong can you be? Vince had been wounded in Iraq. And he was waiting for a desk job at home. He'd had a medal for bravery and everything. His son, Andy, had a dad to be proud of. He wanted to be a soldier like him. I think I was jealous of that. So I hated him too. He hated me all right. I hadn't got that wrong. He was the one who couldn't see why his dad had taken up with my mum... and me.

My mum had said to me, 'Why can't you accept the truth, Logan.' And that was something I never seemed able to do. I built a barrier between myself and reality, and the barrier was Baz. That's how they explain it to me anyway.

The first time they came here to see me together, Vince and my mum, I saw how he cared for her. Cared for me too. How could he care about me, after all the things I'd said to him? We talked and talked and, you know, it was as if a veil had been lifted. I was seeing things clearly for the first time.

They've got a new house now, out in the suburbs. A semi-detached with a garden.

"You'll enjoy it there," Vince said.

But I think it will be a long time before I see that house. I think I may be here for a while. It still frightens me that I spent so much time with someone who didn't exist.

Wouldn't it frighten you?

SIXTY-ONE

Lucie knew. She knew all the time, or at least she suspected, and she tried to tell me.

Did you think she wasn't real either? Don't worry, that scared me as well at first. But no, Lucie's real. She came to see me with her mum, and my mum was there too.

'You're better on your own,' she had said to me more than once. 'Be yourself. Don't blame other people.'

And Baz had told me she was jealous. He was the one who was afraid. The Baz part of me was afraid she knew the truth.

Lucie was worried about me, and she understood. She thought there was nothing too strange about me thinking Baz was real. "I used to have an invisible friend when I was a little girl. You'll grow out of it."

"So, this invisible friend of yours. Did she just disappear?"

She looked at me and smiled with that dimpled smile of hers. "No. I blew her up in the garden shed."

Made me laugh, that did. "You're the one who should be in here, not me."

"Maybe I have been," she said. And I wonder if that is true. Lucie had a hard time before she was finally fostered. Had a lot of problems even afterwards, finding it hard to believe anyone could love her. It took her a long time to settle down, to believe the family she was with really cared about her.

I look forward to her visits. She's the only one who comes. The boys don't. Not Claude. Not Mickey. Not Gary, and I don't blame them. They won't ever want to see me again, I guess, and why should they? If I scared them before when my moods could change so quickly, changing from me to Baz in an instant, how much more would I scare them now – now they know I really thought Baz existed?

Mum tells me the doctors say Claude's legs are going to be ok. It will take a long time, but he's going to be all right. She says that Gary has phoned a couple of times, asking after me. He's a good guy, Gary.

Anyway, I won't be living on the estate with Claude and Mickey and Gary any more, so I won't have to see them. And they won't have to see me.

"Will I ever get better?" I keep asking the doctor. It frightens me that I won't.

She always assures me: "Of course you will. You're going to be fine."

And I think she's right. Writing it all down has helped. I sleep better. I think more clearly. I'm happier.

I am going to be fine.

As long as Baz doesn't come back.

ABOUT THE AUTHOR

Cathy MacPhail is the award-winning author of over thirty children's books including *Run Zan Run*, *Roxy's Baby*, *Out of the Depths* and *Grass*. *Mosi's War* was shortlisted for a 2015 Scottish Children's Book Award, an award Cathy has won twice before, and a film adaptation of her novel *Another Me* was released in 2014. She was born and brought up in Greenock, Scotland, where she still lives.

Cathy has been an ambassador for CHILDREN 1st since 2013. This Scottish charity works with families and communities to improve the lives of children and young people. Cathy is passionate about supporting CHILDREN 1st's work with vulnerable young people.

Visit Cathy's website at catherinemacphail.co.uk
or follow her on Twitter @CathyMacphail